Silver Fairy Tribe

- Prince Nathaniel Shaw
- 1st Wife: Princess Alicia (Deceased)
- 2nd Wife: Princess Rachel Shaw
  - Children:
  - Arabella Shaw and Jeffrey Warner
    - Children:
    - Rolf, Jennifer & Juliette, Antoinette
  - Gwyneth Shaw and Alexander Cann
    - Daniel, Steven
  - Joanna (Deceased)
  - Queen Rebecca (nee Shaw) Lawson and King Hugh Lawson

Featured in:
1) Silver Princess
2) Silver Majesty
3) Silver Verity

Sky Fairy Tribe

- King Jasper Bijou and Queen Marta
  - Children:
  - Prince Oliver and Princess Gemma
    - Children:
    - Jelice
  - Prince Cambrian and Princess Constance (nee Kimberlite)
  - Lesley, Laura, Lila (triplets)

Featured in:
4) Troubled Skies
5) Dress Blues
6) The Seeker's Storm

Wood Fairy Tribe

- King Walter and Queen Fiona
  - Children:
  - Prince Isaac
  - Princess Gallica — engaged to Sir Stuart of Ouray

Featured in:
7) Heartwood
8) Wedgewood
10) Fusion

Water Fairy Tribe

- Muina Region (Central)
  - Regional Speaker Yirri
- Cordus Region
  - Regional Speaker Actare
- Triens Region
- Ten'rae Region
- Sikya Region
- Seyth Region
- Mugan Mugan Region (Outer)
  - Lady Damaris Botere
  - Truth-Seeker Kuntze Botere
  - Doctor Imber Botere

Featured in:
9) Fission

Plant Fairy Tribe

- King Wilson and Queen Dianna

Fission
(Book 9)

by Lea Carter

Copyright © 2020

All rights reserved.

Cover design by Daniel Manfredini.

This is a work of fiction. The characters, names, incidents, places, and dialogue are products of the author's imagination, and are not to be construed as real.

ISBN 978-1-951248-16-1

Fairies to Know

Rolf Warner: youngest Historian in the Silver Fairy Tribe; and oldest nephew of Queen Rebecca of the same tribe.
Approximately sixteen in human terms

Damaris (Mari) Botere: member of the oldest and most powerful Water Fairy family.
Over five thousand fairy years old

Imber Botere: granddaughter to Damaris.
Approximately sixteen in human terms

Katilla Rokoa: mixed heritage; her family has been detained in the seven regions of the Water Fairies for over a hundred generations.
Approximately sixteen in human terms

Elihu Jennings: currently valet to Prince Cambrian of the Sky Fairy Tribe; former windfairy in the Royal Fleet; acting as travelling companion to Rolf Warner.
Approximately three thousand fairy years old

Important places in the Seven Regions

Region Name	Region Capital city:
Muina (Innermost)	Civita
Cordus	Cundi
Triens	Pida
Ten'rae	Lauga
Sikya	Pumed
Seyth	Renna
Mugan (Outer)	Cachora

Chapter 1

Holding his hands under the light of a lightning globe—fist-sized glass baubles that were lit from within—Rolf checked his nails for the fifth time since being shown to the small sitting room. He'd taken pains to clean the ink off his fingers before arriving, but he always seemed to miss a spot. Finding nothing, he clasped his hands behind his back.

The light from the globe was so bright and cheery that he had a hard time remembering the days were bleak and cold outside of the Water Fairy lava tubes where he was spending the winter. In rare places where volcanic magma had cooled and hardened in the seams and cracks of the tubes, colorful fish and plant life danced to the silent, invisible music of the West Sea.

Food and fuel never dwindled here. Neither mosquitoes nor spiders threatened in the depths of the lava tubes where the Water Fairies lived, making it practically perfect.

The one, major drawback in Rolf's mind was that he couldn't fly. Though the Water Fairy tubes crisscrossed the floor beneath the entire West Sea, the tubes and tunnels were simply too narrow to allow the population to fly.

Just thinking about flying made him restless. Turning so that he was facing the longer side of the small, rounded chamber, Rolf tried stretching his wings and stifled a sigh of disappointment when their tips brushed up against the walls. His curiosity satisfied, he withdrew his wings through the carefully tailored slits in his suit coat and folded them against his back.

His silver eyes laughed at his reflection in the highly polished mirror on the wall before him. He was here on assignment from his aunt Rebecca, the Silver Fairy Queen, so he might as well make the best of it.

To take his mind off everything else, he turned his attention to the room where he waited. Something about it bothered him, but what?

Three thinly padded chairs with painfully straight, fishbone backs stood against one wall. And if a guest tried sitting on the plusher divans, they would knock their heads against the frames of some very unfortunately placed paintings. Even the octagonally-shaped table was at an awkward height, too short to graze the top with his fingertips, yet too tall for easy reach should one choose to sit on the near divan.

Yes, that was it. He couldn't help the wry twist of his lips—this room had been appointed specifically for the *discomfort* of its guests. Intentionally, of course.

He couldn't say the room wasn't pretty, though. The eggshell blue paint on the rock walls and ceiling of the chamber brightened things considerably, making it look almost sky-like. Much more pleasant than the stark white of his tiny room at the institute in the library-city of Rutegia.

He made a mental note to suggest painting to his aunt, Queen Rebecca. All surface fairies spent the deadly cold winter months in the safety of enclosed spaces and he knew from personal experience just how demoralizing the dark rooms and rock tunnels of the Silver and Plant Fairies could become.

Wood Fairies solved the problem of 'drab' by wearing bright colors during the winter, often in garish combinations that would cross a wild coorelum's eyes. A little paint on the wooden walls of their tree homes might appeal to them, as well.

Sky Fairies spent the majority of their lives in, on, or around their distant mountain home and he was beginning to wonder how they stood it.

This time he did sigh. *The Sky Fairies.*

Ostensibly, he was at Regalis, the Sky Fairy capital, visiting King Jasper and Queen Marta on official historian business. In reality, he and Prince Cambrian were on royal diplomatic assignment to the Water Fairy Tribe. Thanks to the crazy pirate who tried to steal from a lightning chamber, where lightning was made and stored, they'd proven their peaceful intent quickly enough—though they'd all nearly died in the process.

But the harnessing and manipulation of lightning was only the second-most closely guarded secret of the Water Fairy Tribe. The first was the fact of their existence. He wouldn't even be able to tell his mother the truth of where he'd spent the winter.

Just outside the door to the room where Rolf stood pondering, Damaris Botere paused in the hallway. If her guest looked up, he'd almost certainly see her. The corners of her lips turned down slightly as she considered him. He wasn't much taller than she was, though she could see he still had some growing to do. The cuffs on his tailored suit jacket and yes, even on his trousers, were already riding just a smidge high. No head covering except for his thick, neatly combed silver hair. His shoes had oversized buckles, the only remotely ostentatious piece of his ensemble.

She flicked a gaze at the leather bag that rested on one of her fishbone chairs. At the historian's emblem emblazoned front and center on its cover flap. She'd never doubted her grandson, Kuntza, when he told her Rolf was a Silver Fairy Historian. Not really. She just had a hard time grasping the apparent fact that a sixty-nine year old boy was responsible for transcribing living history. Well over five thousand years old herself, she found herself trying to remember what it was like to be so young. Just starting out on life's journey.

Perhaps it was her soft sigh that caught his attention. Whatever it was, she suddenly found herself staring into two incredibly clear silver eyes. Receiving a friendly, artless smile. She nodded back and entered the room in a stately manner, quite as though she hadn't stopped to study him.

"Good day to you." Rolf bowed slightly to the dignified woman fairy observing him from the hallway. Her charcoal gray dress offset her soft pink hair while the belt around her waist accented her trim figure. Smallish black slippers carried her soundlessly across the room, unlike her calf-length skirt, which swished slightly as she moved. Wise hazel-green eyes assessed him unabashedly from a lovely oval face.

"Good day to you." She greeted him in the common tongue of the surface, then paused. "Historian."

Rolf felt his smile shrink a little. *What would it be like*, he wondered, *to be greeted without preconceptions?* He loved his job, just not the way it made others treat him.

"Please," he invited cordially, "call me Rolf." He itched to relieve his nerves with a violent twitch of his wings, but kept himself from breaking the ensuing silence, from filling it with the chatter he was accustomed to.

"Then you must call me Mari."

He bit his tongue on a reflexive protest. Despite the deceptive freshness of her skin, he knew she was Kuntza's grandmother. Which probably meant she was old enough to be his great-grandmother. Not someone he would ordinarily address so familiarly.

He could hardly refuse a direct invitation, though.

"I would be honored, Mary." He mimicked her pronunciation. Wondering at the amusement that suddenly danced in her eyes, he added, "I bring you Kuntza's heartfelt regrets. As you know, he is helping review certain safety measures in Cachora and isn't able to leave just now." Nobody wanted a repeat of what happened in the chamber where lightning was made and stored in the city of Cachora.

Raising a knowing eyebrow, Mari replied, "Oh yes, I heard all about Amber Bullierd's attempt to hold Cachora hostage." The boy's only response was a slight dropping of his jaw. "In her bid to take over our seven regions for the surface pirates, she disrupted the lightning flow to an entire city, plunging it into darkness," she reminded him gently. "However much the councils would've preferred to keep that a secret, it was a hopeless task from the beginning."

"Yes." Astounded at her command of the common tongue—and at how well-informed she was—Rolf simply nodded. "I was there when it happened." And she was right. Though Cachora's councilors kept most of the details to themselves, though they tried to make a hero out of Princess Constance Bijou of the Sky Fairy Tribe, most of what had happened in the lightning chamber spread across the city before the repairs were completed.

"You're wondering why they haven't released the full story," Mari deduced from the faint crinkles in the young man's brow. Glancing around the uncomfortable room, the only room that unwelcome guests were ever permitted to see, she allowed herself a small smile.

"Come. I have refreshments waiting for you in my lounge." The surface fairy habit of conducting business over food had appalled her when she first learned of it, but a few light snacks seemed a good compromise.

Retrieving his historian's bag, Rolf followed her a tad doubtfully. He still didn't know why Kuntza had called him away from his studies of Water Fairy history. Or what he was doing here, with this enigmatic woman. There were still *rooms* full of history books in Rutegia for him to read before winter ended and he was able to return to the surface.

The Water Fairies had cut themselves off from the surface world eons ago, so whatever knowledge he managed to gain while he was there could only help in hoped-for future interactions.

He'd tried cajoling Jennings, Prince Cambrian's valet and man-of-all-work, into assisting him, but the former Sky Fairy Fleet windfairy had instead chosen to mingle with the 'advena,' as the Water Fairies called the surface fairies they'd imprisoned for 'attempting to infiltrate their domain.'

In the wrong place at the wrong time was more like it from what little Rolf had learned. Victims of windship crashes over the West Sea; prospectors and explorers who ventured too close to hidden portals; that sort of thing.

On the one hand, the Water Fairies hadn't left anyone to die. On the other hand, they hadn't allowed them to leave, either. Once a surface fairy entered the seven regions beneath the sea, they were automatically sentenced to remain there until death freed them.

He might be trapped in the seven regions himself if he hadn't arrived with a letter of introduction from the Silver Fairy King *and* Kuntza Botere, a Water Fairy Truth Seeker, both vouching for him. The Water Fairies had little enough respect for the surface tribes, but thankfully they agreed to trust royal representatives—including Prince Cambrian, Princess Constance, and Jennings, all of whom were of the Sky Fairy Tribe.

"Set the tray on the table," Mari directed her

servant, who arrived precisely as they did. Good. The savory items would still be hot. Discreetly, she looked back at Rolf, who'd been completely silent during their short walk. Not a single question? Not even a remark? How odd. This room never failed to spark a response from her guests on their first visit.

"How do you like your tisane, Rolf?" She was about to seat herself when it happened. Fortunately, she was looking at him squarely and saw his face transform from a polite, if distracted, expression to jaw-dropped awe. Well. That was better.

"This…here?" Rolf stepped further into the room, into the light from the outside world. He hadn't seen anything like this since his initial journey into the seven regions. And they were much deeper here, even though Mugan was the outermost region. "It's…"

Unable to even formulate a complete sentence, he simply stopped talking. Having almost grown accustomed to caverns, chambers, and tunnels underneath the sea, illuminated only by lightning globes, he stared hungrily through the transparent volcanic glass at the shapes and colors darting about in the water over his head, clearly visible through the glass walls and ceiling.

Fish the size of hawks. Shelled creatures the color of sunburned bricks. Turtles as big as mountains, with fins covered in olive green spots. And, in the distance, what looked like a castle. A glowing castle that swayed with the current.

Rolf's legs gave out and he sat abruptly. Ordinarily never more than half an hour from 'starvation,' he looked now at the small spread of treats and dishes without interest.

"Why did you want to see me?" he asked bluntly.

Having decided to forego his tisane, Mari continued preparing a small plate for him as if she hadn't heard.

"Do you like spicy food?" she countered, the tongs hovering over a dish of peppered crab meat.

"Sure." He didn't care if she gave him sugared sawdust, so long as she answered his question.

"Hmm." Mari selected a single piece for him to try. When he had taken the plate, along with a napkin, she smoothed her kelp skirt and seated herself. "I had to see you, Rolf. To speak with you about something that the council has managed to keep a secret." Her lips twitched. "For the most part." She'd retired from her position on a regional council several centuries ago, as had most of her contemporaries. Now, they mentored younger councilors, and as a result, were exceptionally well-informed regarding current events. Also 'non-events.'

"What have I to do with that?" Absent-mindedly, Rolf spread the soft napkin across his thigh.

"Nothing," she answered immediately. "Which we are going to change."

A small wedge of cheese stopped halfway to his mouth. "I beg your pardon?" Surely he hadn't heard her correctly.

"I can forgive them for not thinking of you immediately," she continued. "Before Amber and her pirates, we hadn't had a cocheta—a guest from the surface—for quite some time. Nevertheless." She added spoonsful of herbal powders to a cup, then a pinch of precious sugar and a few ounces of steaming water. Stirring slowly to avoid bruising the flavors, she went on slowly, "As a tribe, we are facing staggering changes. Changes that we cannot prepare for without your help."

Thoroughly bewildered, Rolf did something Princess Arabella, his mother, had taught him years ago. Popping the cheese into his mouth, he chewed slowly, playing for time to think. It should only take him a decade or so to figure out what she meant. He frowned down at his plate, suddenly realizing how small it was. The cheese was delicious.

"I'm going to need more information," he said at last.

Mari allowed herself to relax back against her chair. A thrill of excitement shot through her as she thought of everything she had to tell him. Of course, it was best to begin at the beginning.

"You already know about the treaty."

"The treaty of separation?" Rolf tore a piece off a roll. The last time he'd eaten seemed hours ago! "The one that prohibits the four surface tribes from contacting yours? From even acknowledging that Water Fairies exist, on pain of total extermination? Yes, though I learned of it just recently." He hadn't yet come up with a discreet way to describe the arrangement.

"In the future, I suggest calling it simply the separation." Mari made a mental note to warn him against mocking active council members. They held their dignity dear.

Rolf felt his eyebrows rising in disbelief. "The separation?" he repeated. That sounded a little too…plain for something that could still cause the ruler of a surface tribe to quake in their boots. Silver Fairy, Sky Fairy, Wood Fairy, and Plant Fairy alike.

"Yes." Mari heard the impatience in her tone and took a sip of her tisane to calm herself. What was the matter with her? Had she forgotten so quickly that this was all new to the boy?

"I'll remember that," Rolf promised calmly. In a well-practiced move, he squished the rest of the roll in his hand, then popped it into his mouth. Bite-sized was relative, in his opinion.

Mari took another sip of the soothing liquid, felt it slip down her throat while the orange-vanilla flavor lingered on her tongue.

"So will I," chuckled a deep, familiar voice that had no business being anywhere near the seven regions.

Rolf choked on the roll. A piece of fruit flew off his plate as he fought to cough up the bread. Mari leapt to her feet, but the newcomer reached him first.

"Easy there, lad!" the deep voice ordered as something hard struck him squarely between his shoulders blades. The roll popped out of Rolf's windpipe and joined the fruit on the floor.

Dragging in great gulps of air, Rolf wiped the tears from his eyes and rolled his shoulders. "You pack quite a wallop," he gasped, turning to thank his rescuer.

Mari's lips tightened slightly as the rest of the food—and the plate—hit the floor, bouncing and finally rolling to a stop under chairs, the table, etc. Then she laughed a little.

"Really, Captain Watts." She retook her seat. "I hadn't envisioned such a dramatic entrance for you."

"It *is* you!" Rolf had been convinced he was hearing *and* seeing things, maybe due to oxygen deprivation or something. "But... how?!"

David Watts patted him gently on the shoulder. "I'll tell you everything as soon as we've cleared the deck." He gestured loosely at the spilled food and Rolf's cheeks reddened.

"I'm terribly sorry." Dropping at once to his knees, Rolf set the plate right side up and began rapidly snagging the fallen items. "Such good food, too," he continued apologizing as he moved one knee, putting himself within reach of the rest of it.

Mari's mouth hung open. Not only was she amazed at his prompt and humble reaction, where in the seven regions—no, in *Fairydom*, she corrected herself—had the boy learned to move so quickly?

"Good thing I've had a lot of practice at this." Rolf tried to laugh off his embarrassment. "My little sisters used to spill quite a bit. Especially the twins."

Mari looked over at Captain Watts, who was watching the nimble lad with delight. Sun-bronzed skin crinkled around his clear blue eyes as he grinned and she felt her own lips curving upwards.

"If you hadn't decided to become an historian, Rolf, you'd have done well on a windship. Excellent hand-eye coordination." Captain David Watts swung one leg up and over the nearest short-backed chair.

"I'm ready," Rolf announced, back in his seat almost before the Sky Fairy captain had finished settling himself.

"Well." David blinked. "A lot's happened

since we met aboard the *Falcon* during the pirate offensive. You probably noticed how late winter was this year?" At Rolf's nod, David continued, "Turns out that was because someone was stormpiling the snow clouds. I volunteered to go help clean it up and get the weather back on course."

David ran his fingers through his dark blue hair as memories raced through his mind. The thunder that practically rattled his teeth out of his head. The lightning that nearly killed his navigator. The nerve-wrenching screech of his most recent windship, the *Wind Sorter,* grinding to what was probably her final resting place on the mountainside. "We were doing alright until we touched down at Takoda and found it deserted."

Rolf frowned. "My historian classes include some geography, but I'm not familiar with that town."

Mari chuckled. "It's only inhabited during the warmer months. The miners leave when the weather gets bad and the game is scarce."

"Fortunately for us," David resumed, "we located a cave system. We were moving what supplies we had into it when Mari and I found each other down by the stream that runs through the caves." David smiled, still fascinated by her accented voice. He'd had many a laugh at himself since their first meeting. She'd faked stooped shoulders to make herself look older, feeble even.

"And she brought you here?" Rolf's skepticism stemmed from his own rather peculiar experiences with the tribe. Truth Seeker Kuntza, Mari's grandson, had taken a grave chance when he traveled to Regalis, the Sky Fairy capital. There hadn't been any other way to learn what was really going on before his tribe decided what to do about Amber Bullierd's accusations, though.

"It was not an easy decision," Mari admitted quietly.

"For the first few weeks she supplemented our food supply," David explained, shooting her a grateful look. "Then one of the craftsfairies was trying to patch together a shelter, something to get us up off the rocky floors. A tool slipped and he was injured."

"Badly?" Rolf leaned forward anxiously.

"We would've had to bury him if not for Mari." David regretted his directness when Rolf sat back hastily. "She smuggled him here and got him the best of care. He's made a complete recovery."

Mari, who'd also noticed Rolf's reaction, was puzzled by the way his eyes darted back and forth between herself and David. Did he think they were lying to him?

"After that, I realized I'd been looking at the problem all wrong." Mari picked up the story. "Instead of bringing them all here at once, I sort of drifted them in, two and three at a time like bits of wood on a wave."

Her son, Dilan, hadn't been thrilled with the idea. He'd painted a terrible picture of what would happen should the high council somehow catch onto what she was doing. He wasn't wrong, of course; he'd simply chosen to overlook the fact of how many other lives were at stake. Finding that she was resolved to proceed, he'd wisely gone on a trip to visit his grandchildren in another region. That gave her more room and kept him out of trouble.

"Why are you telling me all this?" Rolf decided to overlook the numerous Water Fairy laws Mari had just admitted to breaking. He didn't know the details, but there was a very particular procedure for handling newly arrived advena.

"Because, as Mari was saying," David smiled at their hostess, "the Water Fairy Tribe needs your help."

"My help?" Rolf took a deep breath. "For what?"

David turned to Mari, who sipped her tisane.

"For generations, we have felt the weight of our injustice to the advena." Mari spoke with quiet earnestness of the surface fairies trapped in the seven regions. "While there did not seem to be any choice in the past, recent events have compelled us to reevaluate. Thanks in large part to the tragedy in Cachora, the high council has agreed that we know far too little of what's happening on the surface. We never should have been taken in by Amber's lies. Therefore, copies of the histories you brought with you from the surface will be distributed to each region—including a special set to be made available to the advena."

Rolf allowed himself a moment of relief that he hadn't any food in his mouth that time.

Chapter 2

"That's wonderful." Astonishing, too. According to Jennings, Water Fairy law forbade the advena to have any books they didn't bring with them from the surface.

"I'm glad you concur."

The smug way she sat back brought Rolf forward, elbows resting on his knees.

"I certainly do. I shall go right back to Rutegia and assist them in making the copies." He waited, curious to see how she would respond to his deliberate twist of her meaning. Instead of hundreds of scribes making copies by hand, Water Fairies used the most amazing machine with separate, moveable letters that they called a 'press.' How he'd love to see it in action! He doubted he would actually get to, unfortunately. Mari seemed to have something quite different in mind for him.

Mari stiffened. Relaxed. "A generous offer, Historian. However," she delicately selected a sweet, dry cracker from the tray, "we were hoping you would personally present the history books to each regional council."

He pondered briefly, trying to think through the situation.

"Perhaps Prince Cambrian would be the better choice for this task?" He held out his hands, palms up. "He's already touring the regions," with his bride, Princess Constance, and her long-lost uncle, whom they'd stumbled upon among the advena, "and is a member of the Sky Fairy Royal Family."

Mari hesitated. "That was suggested," she admitted slowly. "However, because you are an historian, it was agreed that you were the fairy best suited to the task. If you will, that is." Her eyebrows rose ever so slightly.

"Alright now." David waved at nothing to signify clearing the air between them. "Stop fencing, you two. Mari, you could have copies of these books produced and delivered tomorrow like so much baggage if you had a mind to. Rolf knows that and just wants an idea of what's really going on."

Turning to Rolf, he cocked his head to one side. "And once you understand, you'll be glad to help, won't you?"

Amused, Rolf waited for Mari to answer first. She wasn't as accustomed to David's direct manner as he was, and spent several seconds looking dignified while she tried to adjust.

Mari unbent enough to smile at David. "Our friend is correct. The histories will be delivered one way or another. My true purpose in all of this has been to ask you to meet with the councils. To answer their questions, or," she gestured vaguely, "as many as you are able."

Rolf thought he detected a faint stress on her final sentence, as though she was telling the truth, but not all of it. Did the councils need a neutral liaison? They had to have some form of working relationship with the advena in place already, and yet… For such a monumental change in the way things were done, he understood wanting a figurehead of sorts.

"You would like to use me to distract the advena." The words hung in the air between them like a fairy flight training class, wings beating frantically as they tried to stay aloft during an endurance test.

Mari's lips thinned. She didn't deny it. She also didn't say that the advena would be allowed to return to the surface, which was surely what they all wanted. What she wanted for them.

"Will you do it, lad?" David hadn't expected to fool him. Historians had an uncanny way of seeing through things.

"Yes." Rolf straightened in his chair. "I don't know what you're up to, Mari, but I believe you meant what you said about injustice to the advena. If this is some small step forward, I'll support it." Mari opened her lips to respond, possibly in triumph, and he continued speaking anyway. "I cannot guarantee that you will like the results—unless you choose to confide in me."

Mari blinked steadily. Her breaths came at a normal rate and her hazel-green eyes never left his.

"The regional councils have informed me

there are surface historians among the advena. I will arrange for you to meet with them during your visits."

"An excellent idea." Why hadn't she mentioned that sooner? He didn't bother pointing out that they were the most obvious choice for the task of sharing the histories. The matter of why *he* was going, it would seem, was closed. For now.

"I assume you'll be returning to Rutegia?" Mari hesitated, then set her tisane aside and rose.

Rolf came to his feet instantly, in the loose, gangly manner of youth. David stood a tad more slowly, shoulders and back ramrod straight.

"Yes, I'll need to pack a few things." Was there enough paper and ink in all the seven regions to record the history that was about to happen? "And pick up Jennings."

"Jennings?" Mari knew the name only vaguely. "Oh, yes. The third man in your party."

Rolf smiled without meaning to. Somehow, when she said it like that, it sounded like she was planning seating arrangements for a dinner.

"Jennings, eh?" David tugged at his cuffs. He'd had more than a little trouble with the quarrelsome fellow when Jennings was a windfairy aboard the *Nadauld*. "How's he liking life since leaving the Sky Fairy Fleet?"

"Not as much as Cap...um, Princess Constance." Rolf corrected himself hastily. "He's valet to Prince Cambrian now, but since Cambrian's off on his honeymoon, Jennings has taken to spending a lot of time with the advena at Cachora."

"Sounds like he'll be a great help to you," David approved hollowly. Constance had left the Fleet? And married Prince Cambrian, obviously. Not that he should be surprised. She'd as much as told him she loved the prince the last time they'd spoken. Well. She'd make a fine addition to the Sky Fairy Royal Family.

"Very well." For a moment, Mari had expected David to object to this Jennings fellow. Since he hadn't, neither would she. "Muina's regional council will be expecting you in Civita. From there, please work your way outward through the regions to Cachora."

Rolf accepted her instructions with a bow, shook hands with David, and left without a second glance at the remaining snacks.

Racing across town as quickly as his feet would carry him—and longing to fly!—Rolf boarded the next train heading to Rutegia.

Fist-sized lightning globes illuminated the small space, showing that there was only one other fairy in the windowless carriage with him. Hoping to avoid conversation, Rolf moved to the furthest fishbone bench and sat down.

The train took off with a semi-familiar *click*

click click and the whirring of wheels that almost made him miss the racket of the horsefly-drawn wagons back home.

Almost.

This was a much smoother ride, which allowed him to record what had just happened. He stopped himself at a page, because even his best guesses would not be facts.

The train slowed to a stop and the doors to his carriage opened, allowing the other passenger to exit. As Rolf had expected, no one else got on board—but the doors remained open.

A deep voice shouted something from the platform, close enough to his carriage that Rolf wondered what was going on.

A tall Water Fairy guard ducked through the door and scowled at him. "Pres-ent your tra-vel per-mit." The guard ordered awkwardly in the common tongue. He preferred Margua, the language of his own tribe.

Mystified, Rolf took a quick look around the carriage. There was no one else there.

"Me?" Laughing, Rolf ran his fingers through his hair. "Of course me. Sorry, I just..."

"Ne-ver mind your sorries." The guard's narrowed eyes took in what Rolf was doing. Lingered on the paper and ink. "Where did you get those?"

"These?" Rolf held up his pack of spare

quills. "I brought them from Regalis."

"From where?" The guard leaned closer, his grip on his short staff changing in case of trouble.

"Regalis, the Sky Fairy capital city," Rolf explained patiently. Of course the guard wouldn't recognize the name, what was he thinking? "Kuntza told me there would be plenty of quills and ink here, but I like to be prepared."

The guard straightened abruptly, the travel permit forgotten. "Kuntza Botere?"

"Yes." Loud voices outside tugged at Rolf's attention even as he nodded. "I'm Rolf Warner, Silver Fairy historian."

The simple statement of his identity shone like a spotlight on the situation. Advena weren't allowed to travel without permits. They were also prohibited from making books. With all of his writing supplies, it might look as if he was flouting the law. Granted, he was a cocheta, a guest from the surface, but how was a guard supposed to know that at a glance? The first thing they would see was his silver hair— and respond accordingly.

A burly guard with thick pink hair swaggered aboard and came to join his comrade. "Giving you trouble?" His tone implied that he certainly hoped so.

"No. No trouble." The tall guard glanced again at the paper and ink, then pointed at Rolf's bag. "I need to see that."

"Of course." Rolf lifted the bag from the bench beside him, displaying the embroidered historian crest.

"Thank you." Satisfied with what he saw, the tall guard turned to leave.

The burly guard glared at him. "We must con-fis-cate these things."

"No." The answer was instant and sharp as a razor blade. "Tra-vel well, His-torian Warner."

"Thank you." Rolf did his best to pretend he wasn't interested in the following drama, but dearly wished he could hear the angry, whispered conversation between the two guards.

The doors closed behind them and someone on the platform shouted in Margua.

Just like that, the train resumed travelling toward its final stop and Rolf's destination of Rutegia.

A lump formed in his throat. Mari had mentioned their injustice to the advena. Yes, there was definitely injustice, and he was now party to it. As an advena, the survivor of some calamity that brought him here, his things would've been taken from him and he most likely would've been questioned as to where he'd obtained them. He might even have been detained during an official investigation of the matter.

Since he was Historian Rolf Warner, a rare

cocheta from the surface, he'd simply been patted on the head and told to go play.

Closing his eyes, he sat back to think. He *knew* it made sense. The laws concerning advena were strict because if even one advena escaped to the surface, the existence of the Water Fairy Tribe would be revealed. The advena might or might not be believed if they told their stories, but the Water Fairies couldn't risk that.

As the train rolled into the station at Rutegia, Rolf sighed. No matter how many times he told himself that the guards had good reason to patrol trains for advena this close to the surface—Rutegia was in the Seyth region, only one in from Mugan—he still chafed under the knowledge that he'd been given what felt like special treatment.

Exiting the carriage, Rolf looked around hopefully and was pleased to see a cart with the institute's emblem parked by the supply carriage.

"Historian Warner, good day to you." An older man touched his forehead deferentially, his fading green hair bobbing with the motion.

"Cularos." Rolf recognized him as a cook from the institute. "How are you?" Without waiting to be asked to help, he grabbed one of the heavy vegetable crates off the train and placed it in the back of cart.

"Here, here." Cularos protested, reaching out

to stop him as he returned for another crate. "You can't do that!"

"Why not?" Rolf transferred a second crate, then respectfully paused to listen. "You shouldn't have to do it by yourself, Cularos."

"I'll…I'll bring a boy with me next time." The older man wiped his mouth nervously. "Only please. Let me do my work."

Rolf leaned on the stack of crates. "Why, Cularos? Are you afraid they'll think you're too old? You're still the best cook at the institute, with probably another millennium before anyone would seriously suggest you retire." Truthfully, fairy longevity had an interesting way of making things difficult. How did one fill nine or ten thousand years?

Cularos fingered the buttons on his coarse brown vest and shook his head. "You do your work, Historian. Let me do mine."

Reluctantly, Rolf moved aside. While Cularos transferred the heavy crates of food, Rolf formulated and discarded questions, looking for the right place to start the conversation he wanted to have.

Finally, as they rode the hand-powered cart along the side track to the institute, Rolf ventured to ask, "Where were you born, Cularos?"

"The third region, in the city of Arrena."

"Did you have work there?" Rolf kept his tone as casual as possible. How many of the advena were born here, in one of the seven regions? Would they even be interested in the surface histories?

"Yes, we had good work there."

"Will you tell me about it?"

"I won't cause trouble." Cularos shifted on the seat, putting more space between them.

"Trouble? What do you mean?" Nonplussed, Rolf stared at him.

"We had good work there," Cularos insisted stubbornly.

Rolf couldn't get another word out of him the rest of the trip. Not even about what was for supper.

Relief washed over him when the institute came into sight at last, a squat building originally built to house a small library. The coloring of the fishbones it was carved from made it easy to tell the relative ages of the sections that meandered around the edge of the cavern—the newer bones were still white from being cast up on the beach and bleached by the sun before being salvaged.

As they reached the student quarters, Rolf slipped the strap of his bag over his head. Smiled sadly at Cularos. "I wasn't trying to cause trouble, my friend. I just don't know what kind of work there is to do in the third region." Waving farewell, he jumped off the cart and flew a few flaps to land lightly on the ground.

It felt good to stretch his wings! The tunnels and caverns of the seven regions were so bursting with fairies that it wasn't safe to fly. Not without extensive planning on how to keep the fliers from crashing into and hurting each other.

He kept up with his wing exercises, but that was all he generally had room for.

At Castlemain, the Silver Fairy capital city, he would've flown right up to and through his window, soaring like a spring breeze. Here, every step of the two flights of stairs that he had to climb made his heart sink even further. What had he gotten himself into this time?

It was his own fault, of course. He could've said no when his aunt asked him to come visit the Water Fairies. Even if she was the queen of the Silver Fairy Tribe, she would've heard him out. Sent someone older. Wiser.

Squeezing past the door of his room, Rolf shut it behind him so he could open the dresser drawers. Lifting out his clothes, he tucked them into a soft-sided travelling bag and set it on the spare bed. He'd arrange to store his notes from his studies there while he was gone, which hopefully wouldn't be too long.

Stretching out on, he threaded his fingers together and set them behind his head while he stared up at the ceiling.

Truthfully, he was torn. Now that he'd spent some time in the seven regions, he wished with every fiber of his being that the advena were free to come and go as they pleased. On the other hand, for that to happen the Water Fairy Tribe would have to make itself known—which meant he should be studying their history even more earnestly so he could help with the reintegration.

He definitely should not be leaving his studies to *make* history.

Again.

Frustrated, he scrubbed a hand over his face. Sky Fairy, Plant Fairy, Wood Fairy, or Silver Fairy, historians rarely made even the footnotes of their own work. Most of them lived quiet lives in one city or another, recording major events. But not him.

A knock at the door brought him up on his elbows.

"Come in."

"Message for Historian Warner." An arm reached through the narrow opening, waving a folded piece of paper.

"Thank you." Hopping up, Rolf took it with a light laugh. "Wait, if you please. I may need to send a response."

As he'd expected, it was from Mari. Who else? Copies of the history books would be delivered to the train yards in each region, awaiting his arrival.

Interesting. Underlying her polite wording was the strong implication that they were expecting him to start sooner rather than later.

"Any response?"

"Hmm?" Coming back to himself, he answered, "Oh, no, thank you."

Checking the clock on the wall, he confirmed that the trains had stopped running for the day. It was just as well. He needed to travel back to first and talk with Jennings anyway. If he was lucky enough that his friend agreed to come along, Jennings would have to pack, tie up any loose ends, and so forth before he was ready to leave.

Better to get a fresh start in the morning.

In the meantime, he dug out the train map booklet. Ate an apple and some cheese while he worked. Apparently, he was to start in the central region of Muina and work his way out. And Muina's capital city was…Civita.

He couldn't begin to estimate how long each visit would take, so he concentrated on calculating the time for the journey itself. Sat back and blew out a breath. The inter-regional train lines ran directly between supply points instead of between capital cities. He'd have to transfer to a regional line every single time.

"It's going to take days to travel between these cities. Amounting to weeks as I backtrack, wait for trains, sleep…" Dejected, he tossed his pencil onto the bed. "Maybe things'll look better in the morning."

They didn't. A hot breakfast usually put him

in high spirits, but today even jackfruit waffles with saso flower syrup couldn't make him smile.

Then, as he exited the train at Cachora, he bumped into a friend.

"Historian Warner." Councilor Naydie greeted him in her pleasantly accented common tongue. "Back so soon?"

"Sooner than I expected." Since they were walking the same direction, he offered her his arm. He looked around for Kuntza and was surprised not to see him. Odd. He'd gotten the distinct impression that Kuntza and Naydie had begun seeing each other socially weeks ago. After the, um, catastrophe in the lightning chamber got sorted out.

"You were so excited when you found out about Rutegia, I imagined you'd be there for months, up to your elbows in decaying scrolls and dusty old records." She shuddered lightly, but smiled to show she was teasing.

He chuckled. "That was the plan." He'd almost been disappointed at how neat and tidy the library was, though. Every document was on a strict schedule of preservation, but simply put, their seaweed paper stayed in good condition longer than the wood-based paper he was accustomed to.

Naydie tugged on his arm, redirecting them down a side tunnel. One with noticeably less foot traffic.

Sensing that she wanted to talk with him

more seriously, Rolf followed her lead. It explained why she just 'happened' to be at the train station when he arrived. As an active member of Cachora's city council, she probably knew more about what was going on than he did. He certainly hoped that was the case.

"How's Kuntza doing?" To his amusement, she looked away and smoothed her hair. He had the worst luck. He escaped his newlywed aunt and uncle-by-law at Castlemain only to have Prince Cambrian marry Constance. They left to travel the seven regions and voila, Kuntza started courting Naydie.

"He's well." She casually looked over her shoulder. "If you're looking for Jennings, he's been spending a lot of time in the marketplace."

"I was about to go hunting him, yes." He frowned, not liking her tone. "Is something wrong?"

"Probably not. Ever since Wynston left with his niece, Princess Constance, there's been sort of a…" She let go of his arm to motion with her hands, as if she could conjure up the word she sought. "A gap. The advena here looked to him for leadership."

"I see." They turned left, away from his rooms. Not toward the market, either. She must have a lot to say.

"The council was always able to work with Wynston, Rolf. He was an instigator, almost a trouble-maker, in his younger days, but he's done well for centuries now."

"Done well?" he interrupted.

"Yes. He's been a law-abiding advena, living peaceably." They paused to let a delivery cart go by, then walked across an intersecting tunnel. "We value the good example he sets for the others."

"Oh." Rolf frowned as a thought occurred to him. "What happens to the advena who *don't* do well?"

She flushed. "I'm not sure I like your tone, Rolf."

"Can't say that I like what I'm hearing." He stopped walking and raked his fingers through his hair, causing the longer part in front to come down over his eyes in a screen of silver. Ugh, what a time to realize he needed a haircut.

"Rolf." She touched his arm lightly. "You haven't even been here a full season. You can't really believe you know everything about our way of life."

After a brief internal struggle, his shoulders slumped. "No, I don't believe that."

"If we can't let the advena go," her eyes grew sad, "and they refuse to behave peaceably, we have no choice but to separate them from those they would harm."

"Speak plainly, Naydie." He sighed and pinched the bridge of his nose between his fingers. "Are they in prison?"

"Prison?" Her face scrunched up as she tried

tried to interpret the word. Most of the advena clung to the common tongue, making it advisable for councilors to learn to speak it, but this was not a term she was familiar with.

"Are they confined? Kept in small rooms by themselves?"

Chapter 3

"What a dreadful thought! No, no of course not. Who would do such a thing?" The horror on her face made him feel foolish for asking.

He wished he could hide his face as he mumbled, "We do."

Wide-eyed, she stared up at him. "Perhaps the surface is not as peaceful as we were led to believe."

"It is," he insisted. He was one of those that had testified to that fact. "I'm not talking about intertribal warfare or pirates, I'm just…" Pivoting mentally, he turned the tables on her. "Are there no Water Fairy lawbreakers? Fairies that need to be separated for the protection of others?"

She cringed. "It rarely comes to the level of separation you describe. For *any* fairy."

"We're not so different, then." Wait. Was he telling her? Or himself?

Her eyes searched his and she nodded slowly. "Mari chose well."

Before he could regroup his thoughts after her startling remark, she had resumed walking.

"We were talking about Jennings."

Had they been? He searched back through his memory of their conversation and realized she was right. He felt like he'd run a mental marathon and was now being asked to walk 'just a few feet more' because someone moved the finish line.

"You'll most likely find him with the weavers. When he decides to go with you, I'd appreciate it if you'd ask him to give this," she handed over a folded sheet of paper, "to the wisest advena leader." With that and a nod, she turned off into a main tunnel and merged with a flood of sedately walking Water Fairies.

He studied the paper for a moment, then checked the directional markers etched into the rock walls at the intersection. Somehow, his thoughts made his feet feel like lead as he trudged toward the market.

The long walk gave him time to sort through at least some of what he was feeling. Sharing surface history with the advena was still moving things in the right direction, so he again concluded that he would help with that. Other lines of thinking raised more questions than answers until he gave up and just put one foot in front of the other.

The air current changed subtly as he approached the market, shifting from bringing him the smells of the train yard and production districts to the delightful aromas of various hot foods from the market eateries.

Once more, the prospect of food failed to improve his mood. The tame air currents here were a poor substitute for the free, fresh breezes at home. For the wind in his face as he took his flying lessons. His wings twitched with the urge to be in motion.

Slowly, he came to himself enough to notice that the foot traffic around him was changing. Pale pink, dark pink, shocking pink, short, long, and curly pink hair gave way to variety as relative silence yielded to a hustle and bustle.

Brown-haired Wood Fairies and their delivery carts rumbled past as he stepped into the enormous cavern that housed the market. Colorful tents stretched as far as the eye could see, interspersed with booths and stalls hawking a wonderful assortment of goods.

The shouts of green-haired Plant Fairy descendants echoed as they called their wares, drawing him to their stalls at the edge of the colorful chaos.

"How much for one of those?" He pointed at a bag of roasted burr nuts. Kuntza, recognizing that Rolf would need spending money, had graciously provided him with a small stipend.

"One llow." The vendor placed a small weight on his scales, preparing to complete the sale.

"One llow?" Rolf fumbled in his belt pouch for the gold cubes Water Fairies used as currency. Llows were roughly the size of a fingertip and often hard to find in a cluttered pouch. "Um…I'm all out of those."

The vendor shrugged and returned the weight to its box. He'd already offered it at the sale price; he couldn't afford to give it away.

"How many will you give me for a hagax?" Rolf jokingly produced a thumb-sized rod of solid gold. They were worth quite a bit and consequently, he found that they were the hardest to spend.

"You could buy half his stand for that," muttered a neighbor.

"Where'd you get it?" asked another vendor suspiciously.

"I…" Rolf moved back a smidge, not liking the way they were looking at him. He'd never been so innocent and felt so guilty in all his days.

"Is all well here?" A guard appeared at his elbow, pink hair peeking out from under his black, peaked officer's cap.

"It is." Rolf hated to see the way the vendors faded back to their booths, eyes still on him but leery of the guard. He would have preferred to clear the matter up. Except none of these vendors would sell him anything now. "Perhaps you can help me, though."

"Help you?" The guard's hand strayed toward the whistle that hung from his neck. One blast from it would bring guards from all over the market. Two blasts would bring them running, staffs at the ready.

"Yes." Rolf continued hastily. "I wanted to

buy some of these fine burr nuts, but I don't have any llows. Could you trade out a hagax for me?"

"I don't carry that much currency on duty." The guard laughed a little. "There's a changer over this way. Come, I'll show you where to find his booth."

"Thank you." Rolf glanced sideways at the vendors and found their eyes still glaring at him as he walked away. Because he'd been friendly with the guard? Or because of the money? Or…both?

"If you'll take a word of caution," the guard spoke casually, "you'll not be so free with telling folk you're carrying hagax."

"I think you're right," Rolf agreed glumly. He made a mental note to thank Kuntza for his generosity and ask if he could only get half of his stipend next time. He didn't spend it fast enough. Of course, that might change now that he was going to be doing so much travelling. He shook his head at his own indecision.

The guard stopped and indicated the changer's booth with a jerk of his chin.

"Thanks."

"By the way." The guard's voice hardened. "Where *did* you get that hagax?" While pickpouches weren't common in Cachora, the way they were in the inner regions, he'd never live it down if he had one and let him go.

"Kuntza Botere gave it to me." Rolf was

really, really sorry he'd spoken to anyone for the last two days. Life was so much simpler in the libraries of Rutegia.

"Why?" The guard's eyes narrowed. He knew the zaldun's family was wealthy, but he hadn't heard that they were giving money away to advena.

"Because he felt sorry for the visiting cocheta." Wearily, Rolf turned to show the crest on his jacket shoulder.

"Historian Warner." The guard nodded in recognition and touched the brim of his cap deferentially. Thought he'd never have recognized the young man from the descriptions in the wild tales, the embroidered mark matched perfectly.

As Rolf turned away from the guard, he once more felt the prick of guilt. The advena were constantly under suspicion.

"Lad, you look like someone stole your dessert." A heavyset man with thick brown hair and hard green eyes grinned up at him from behind a canvas-topped table. "I'm Narius. What seems to be the trouble?"

"I, um…" Rolf glanced around, surprised to realize that the changer was positioned a discreet distance away from any other booths.

Poles the height of a man were spaced evenly around the edges of the booth. Brightly colored, embroidered scrolls hung from each pole, simultaneously advertising the changer's presence and making accidental observation more difficult for passersby.

"I need to change some Water Fairy currency," Rolf managed to finish.

The man smirked and gestured at the table. "Is there any other kind?"

Rolf innocently opened his mouth to mention surface currency, but decided against it. He'd had enough trouble for one day.

"Good point," he returned instead. Warily, he set a single hagax on the table. The man's eyes widened until they were in danger of popping out of his head, prompting Rolf to close his pouch. He'd find somewhere else to change the other hagax.

"Haven't seen one of these in quite a spell." Narius hefted the hagax and nodded, then set it on his scales anyway. "Can't be too careful," he apologized when the weights tallied. "Had a run of hollow hagax once."

"That's terrible!" Alerted, Rolf watched closely to make sure Narius didn't pull a switch of his own by removing or replacing any of the weights.

"How were you wanting it back?" Narius pulled a wheeled chest of drawers over to him.

"Llows, please."

Narius spread his hands. "I can't give you all my llows, friend. And even if I did, you'd still have some llowtxi coming. How about this?" He opened the middle drawer. "Half in llow, a fourth in llowdia, and whatever's left in llowtxi?"

"That's fine." Rolf shrugged, a little lost. He knew the llow was worth the least and the llowdia worth the most, so he thought it probably made sense to give the difference in the medium-sized cube, the llowtxi. Probably.

"Let's get started." Rubbing his hands together, Narius set the hagax aside and put a larger plate on the scales. "We'll need the extra room," he explained solicitously.

Rolf carelessly picked up the hagax, twirled it in his fingers, and set it on the larger plate. As he'd feared, that side now weighed more than its opposite scale, meaning it would've taken less than the value of a hagax to make the sides appear to balance.

"My mistake." Narius smiled thinly, knowing he'd been caught trying to cheat Rolf.

"Easily fixed." Rolf selected another small weight and added it to the group opposite the hagax. The needle in-between the plates centered itself.

"Easily." There was a slightly oily quality to Narius's smile now, but he measured out the change without hesitation.

Then, when Rolf reached out to collect it, Narius caught him by the wrist.

"There's the small matter of my fee, friend."

"Your fee?" Rolf released the cubes and

Narius released him. "You said nothing about a fee." He suddenly became aware of a thickly-muscled man standing just outside the ring of scrolls. Watching him.

"In the future, I reckon you'll remember to settle the fee first." Jennings appeared out of nowhere. Putting his elbow on Rolf's shoulder, he leaned heavily on him. "Before you show the changer what you've got."

Rolf felt like a fool, but he just nodded.

"Being as we're all friends here." Jennings shoved his blue hair out of his face. "I'm sure Narius'll make you a good deal."

"Friends, is it?" Narius leaned back and indulged in an unprofessional scowl.

"To be sure." Jennings wrapped his arm around Rolf's shoulders and gave him a squeeze that nearly lifted him off his feet. "We came from the surface together."

Curiosity replaced some of Narius's ire and he looked Rolf over. "That explains a lot." He took back a single llowdia.

Rolf waited, then took the plate and poured it into his pouch, which bulged with the bulk.

"Outstanding." Jennings had the audacity to pat Narius on the arm. "Don't worry, we'll spend it all here." He gestured at the market in general.

They hadn't gotten ten steps from the booth when Jennings dragged Rolf into a poorly lit tent and hissed, "Pass over half of that loot, you wee fry. A pouch that size will only draw the wrong attention.”

“Sorry.” Flushing, Rolf did as he was instructed. “What’s a fry?”

Jennings rolled his eyes and used a llow to buy something from the tent’s proprietor.

“You’ll have to pardon my language. I’m starting to speak like these poor fellows.” He gestured at the advena in general.

“You’re pardoned.” Rolf bumped him with his shoulder, relieved to be with a friend again. “What’s a fry?”

Chuckling, Jennings explained. “Correctly speaking, it’s the word for a baby fish. Hereabouts, it’s what folks call young’uns.”

“And the inexperienced.” Rolf laughed with him. “I suppose that’s fair.” Squinting at Jennings, he asked, “But did you do it right the first time you dealt with a changer?”

“No, lad.” Jennings bumped him back. “Can’t say as I did.” Pointing at an open area in front of them, he suggested, “I eat here whenever I can. Food’s nearly as good as at home, but as you might imagine, it’s fairly expensive. Since what I carry is rightfully yours…”

“You’ve appealed to my curiosity.” Rolf gave a ‘lead on’ sweep of his arm. “Let’s eat!”

“Katxa!” Jennings bellowed, dragging out the ‘saw’ sound at the end of her name and turning every head in the vicinity. “Set a plate!”

Rolf flinched, then elbowed him. "I thought you didn't want to draw attention to us?"

Rubbing his ribs, Jennings bellowed again, "Make that two plates!" In a lower voice he told Rolf, "But I do want to call attention to the eatery, lad. Can you think of a better way to advertise it?"

"Stop your yellin', you heathen!" A young woman with twinkling brown eyes and braided green hair poked her head around the edge of the kitchen wall. "Find a seat and I'll be right out."

"Close your mouth, lad, or you'll start lookin' like a fish, too."

Rolf snapped his mouth shut and sat down across from Jennings at a worn, fishbone table. Tried to ignore the way Jennings was snickering at him.

"Pretty, ain't she?"

"Right, then." Katxa plunked down two empty tankards and a pitcher of…something Rolf didn't recognize. Fists on her hips, she asked Jennings, "What'll you have?"

"Two plates of your best brisket, taters, rolls, and whatever vegetable you might have that wasn't grown in the wet." The order rattled off Jennings' tongue easily, as if he'd placed it often enough that she should've known it.

"'Tis always the same with you." Katxa cocked her head at Rolf. "Would you like to place your own order, sir? We have the best crab cakes and shrimp in the market."

"Another time, thank you." He swallowed and willed away the tadpoles kicking around in his stomach. "Brisket sounds delicious."

She tsked, but went off to get what they'd asked for.

"It's the most expensive thing they offer," Jennings muttered, then patted his pouch. "You're sure?"

"Now you ask me." Rolf shrugged. "I'm starving and I haven't had beef since I left for Rutegia."

Jennings grimaced. "Sorry about that, lad. Must've been bad overall, eh?"

"No, it was amazing—if you don't count the food."

"Well, what brought you back if you liked it so well?" Jennings' forehead crinkled in confusion.

"Oh." His appetite faded as he remembered. Everything. "I've got to do something." In light of this new task, Kuntza's stipend suddenly didn't seem like a gift anymore.

"And you need my help, right?" Jennings smirked.

"Right!" Rolf watched the smug smile fade.

"Must be a strange sort of something."

"Here we are." Katxa brought their orders and a wink for Rolf. "Eat hearty!"

Rolf lifted his fork with a nod of thanks and dug in. Thankfully, Jennings let him eat in peace, because the brisket was perfect.

"Here, Katxa." Jennings dropped handful of cubes into her palm and pulled Rolf to his feet.

"No dessert today?" She stirred the cubes with her finger, counting them out of habit. There were two extra llow.

"Maybe tomorrow." Jennings had an odd hunch that wasn't going to happen. A funny itch in his wings like change was coming his way.

Rolf let Jennings steer him to a peaceful spot partway up a slope that gradually rose into one side of the cavern's walls.

"What's got you so quiet, lad?" Jennings plopped himself into a chair someone had carved out of the dark rock. Ruefully investigated a worn spot in the sole of his favorite pair of boots. Blasted seven regions. He had to walk everywhere and never on soft dirt or wood planking.

"It's kind of complicated." By the time he'd finished relating what he'd been asked to do, Jennings had gone still.

"That's…quite a reversal." He scratched his jaw, cursing the quirk of nature that gave him itchy afternoon stubble. "Up till now they've always discouraged the galdu from being too curious about the surface."

"The gal-doo?" That was a new word for Rolf.

"Aye. The Water Fairies call them advena." Jennings looked out over the market. "They call themselves the galdu tako. The lost tribe."

"A sixth tribe?"

"Aye. If you think about it, they're right. On the surface, marrying between tribes is rare. Just ain't that much interaction, except on the trade routes or maybe the diplomatic corps. Down here, it's a whole different world. Their origin tribes don't hardly exist anymore for these folk." Wasn't a bad way to live, so far as he could tell.

"I see what you mean." Rolf massaged his forehead. "That sort of complicates my job, doesn't it?"

"How so?"

"Well, if they're not interested in the surface, how can I teach them about it?"

"Oh, they're interested." Jennings rested his elbows on his knees and his chin on his fists. "When the tents are closed and the chairs put up and everyone's gone home for the night, the wee ones gather about their eldest kith, the family akoa, to hear stories about the surface."

It was easy for Rolf to imagine that, having grown up listening to stories told by his grandparents and their parents and grandparents.

"You've heard some of these stories." At

Jennings' nod, Rolf studied his hands. "Is there any truth to them?"

The whole reason for historians was that things had a way of getting distorted over time. Not intentionally. But especially in the case of stories, where there was an audience to entertain, to astound, to enthrall—well, it was understandable, really.

"You'd be impressed." Jennings held up his hand when Rolf started to frown. "I mean it. The stories are old, some too old even for the most ancient of their akoa to have experienced, but the ones I've heard were all as accurate as a textbook."

"How is that possible?" Now Rolf *really* wanted to meet the adve…um, galdu tako historians. He'd grant that these weren't sworn historians. Nevertheless, they were clearly filling the role.

"Simple, once you know how. They memorize them." Jennings held out his hand near his bended knee to indicate the height of a child. "Tell the stories to all of them as wee ones, then teach the exact wording to the ones what have the will to do it."

"I've never heard of anything like it," Rolf admitted. The feat of memory Jennings was describing earned them high marks in his book.

"I'd take you to a kontatz tonight, but from what you've said we'd best be on our way." He started to rise, then hesitated. "Something you ought to know. No matter what story the akoa tells, every kontatz ends the same way. With a promise that they'll return to the surface someday."

Chills rippled through Rolf.

"Do you think they ever will?" Jennings sounded hopeful and doubtful at the same time.

"What do you think?" Rolf dropped the question back in his lap.

"Hard to say." He tugged on his ear lobe. "The Water Fairies have things buttoned up so tight a galdu family needs a permit to go to anywhere but further into the regions."

"Away from the surface." Rolf interjected without thinking.

Jennings nodded and continued, "This morning I reckon I woulda said they'd never make it. But now, I'd say there's room to wonder."

Rolf's mind churned with the possibilities. Was *that* the true Water Fairy motivation? Ease up here a little, there a smidge, toss in a surface historian for a distraction, then poof—everyone go home?

His head was going to explode.

Chapter 4

Jennings was the first off the train when it whirred to a stop in Civita the next morning.

"Can't stand that windowless crate," he grumbled as he moved clear of the crowd of fairies eager to climb aboard. He scratched at his chest and stretched. Snorted. "Man can't get a wink of sleep with those lightning globes all bright in his face, either."

"You just slept for nine hours," Rolf retorted, glumly wiping at the ink on his fingers. He had a harder time sleeping on the painfully stiff benches than his friend. "At least it's a smooth ride. I got my history book mostly updated." Finding the right words to explain about the advena calling themselves the 'galdu takoa' hadn't been easy. As far as he knew, this was a first for the history books.

"Well, I'm hungry." Jennings slapped his flat stomach, somehow producing a hollow sound. "Let's find an eatery."

"After we find somewhere to sleep." It might be mid-morning, but Rolf was in no mood to meet the council just yet. Chuckling dryly, he smoothed his tunic and gestured at the city map painted on the wall near the opening of the walking tunnels. "Maybe we'll get lucky and find both."

Jennings grumbled while Rolf consulted the

map.

"Look." Rolf tapped a spot. "The lodging area is only one tunnel away from their eateries."

"Huh." Jennings grabbed both of their packs and slung them over his shoulder, waving away Rolf's protest. Together they weighed less than half a cannonball. "C'mon, then. Time's a-wastin'."

"Do you notice anything weird about this map?" Rolf asked, leaning against the wall a moment longer.

"You can't eat it?" Jennings snickered at his own joke, then humored the lad. "Ain't much of a city, is it? Not so much as a metalsmith listed there."

"Exactly. No manufacturing of any sort." Rolf tapped the train station at the center of the map. "Libraries. Shops. Residential areas. A bilera. A market."

"And eateries, if you've a mind to find 'em." Jennings tugged at his arm. "I'll buy you a map tomorrow, but I can't do that if I starve t'death today."

Laughing, Rolf fell in beside him. "I've just never seen such a city. Even Castlemain has an industrial section. There's just so much to do. Hides to tan, food to process, wood to cut…" He hand-shrugged once he figured he'd made his point.

"Maybe that's why they's so many shops here."

Jennings kept both eyes open for the cross tunnel they were after. "If they don't make what they need, they have to buy it."

"Yes, I see your point, but…" Rolf scratched his head, perplexed. "Where do they get the funds to buy all that they need?"

"Rolf, you're a good lad and I like you. But sometimes you think too much like a…well, like the Silver Fairy that you are. Aha!" Jennings took the tunnel to the right and began walking faster. "Almost there."

"I guess I do." Rolf punched Jennings lightly on the shoulder. "Can't help trying to figure things out." Sighing in relief, he headed for the first building he saw that boasted a sign ending with 'inn.'

"Too close to the station, lad. It'll either be full or pricey. Come along a bit further." Grinning, Jennings blocked him from going in.

"Good point." Rolf followed Jennings past the next three inns, then tried to stop again.

Jennings objected each time Rolf tried to turn in until they finally came to the last—and smallest—building in the row. The sign hanging from the building read, 'The Sequoia.'

"This one!" Jennings held out his hands, then rubbed them together. "It's perfect."

The steps carved into the foundation piece of fishbone led up to a three-story building. Every visible window had curtains, but the bottom floor windows were uncovered, allowing them to see inside. Two chairs flanked a small table that had a short stack of books on it. The brightly colored carpet and wall hangings were very appealing after the drab train and tunnel.

"You wanted this one the entire time, didn't you?" Rolf asked flatly.

"To be sure." Jennings straightened his vest and smoothed his hair.

"Why didn't you just say so?!" he fumed. Then… "Are you prinking?" Rolf couldn't believe his eyes.

"You only get one first impression, lad." Jennings even went so far as to rub the toes of his boots on the backs of his pants legs before opening the door.

Rolf hesitated. Checked his own appearance. His simple gray and tan traveling clothes would never do for dinner at court, but… He shrugged and walked inside.

"Two of your very best rooms, if you please." Jennings was instructing the portly man behind the counter.

"Jennings." Rolf glared at his friend, then turned to examine the prices listed on the wall. They hadn't walked this far to get rooked now. "One room with two beds, please."

Jennings held up his hand, making the man pause as he reached for a key.

"We've had a hard trip, haven't we?"

"A hard trip?" Rolf squinted at him. This

from the man who'd lived half his life on the wind, sleeping in a hammock in a tiny hold shared with…with Rolf didn't know how many other windfairies? "Are you feeling well?" He continued protesting, albeit in a lowered tone, as Jennings pulled him away from the desk. "I've had more strenuous picnics!"

"What you don't seem to understand," Jennings growled softly, "is that this inn belongs to Erdi Rokoa. His is one of the most powerful galdu families in the seven regions."

"Alright, fine, we'll stay the night here." Rolf folded his arms across his chest. "But I'm not spending an entire hagax for one night's lodging!" Inwardly, he was glad he hadn't contacted Kuntza yet. He could only imagine the prices at the local eateries.

"Who's to say how long we'll be here?" Jennings countered.

"What?" Confused, Rolf stared at him. "That's not the right way to convince me to get the more expensive option!"

"Can I help you gentlemen?" a distinctly feminine voice asked. "I understand there's some problem about the price?"

"No problem at all." Jennings smiled over Rolf's shoulder.

Irritated, tired, and apparently hungrier than Jennings, Rolf turned to face the speaker. His heart did a funny little jig at the sight of a lovely, green-haired, blue-eyed woman. She was approximately his own age, give or take a decade.

"Katxa?" he asked, astonished. What was the waitress from the Cachora eatery doing here? No, wait. Katxa had *brown* eyes. The eyes watching him curiously were the same shape and in a very similar face, but this was definitely not Katxa.

"I am Katilla Rokoa, sir. I manage this inn for my father." The young woman stepped down off the last stair and released the skirts she'd been demurely holding. "Do you know my younger sister, Katxa?"

"We do." Jennings cheerfully ventured into the silence. "She sent a note for you." He produced an envelope with a flourish and a half bow.

"How…?" Rolf stopped himself mid-question. It wasn't any use to ask how Jennings had gotten the note without making a second stop at the eatery. Spotting the name written on the envelope as it changed hands, he automatically made a mental note of the unusual spelling as compared with how she pronounced it, Ka-tea-ya.

"Oh, thank you." Katilla favored Jennings with a warm smile as she tucked the note in a sleeve pocket to read later. "You must be her friend, Jennings. She's written me so much about you."

Rolf stared, slack-jawed, as she took Jennings'

elbow and led him to the desk.

"The key to the Meranti Suite, please," she instructed the man behind the counter.

"How much does that cost?" Rolf hated sounding like a cranky old ant trader, but they had limited funds. Come to think of it, how would Kuntza know where to send his next week's stipend?

Katilla's answering smile made him feel warm all over, which only served to confuse him further.

"For Katxa's friends, we will make a special rate." Katilla wriggled her fingers a trifle impatiently at the clerk. "The price of a single room."

"I rented the Meranti suite just an hour ago, Miss Katilla," the clerk apologized. Smiling hopefully, he held out a key anyway. "Will the Mountain Ash Suite be alright?"

"Sounds great to me." Jennings grinned.

Rolf's irritation, which had begun to subside under Katilla's gentle influence, grew rapidly at Jennings' smug answer. So much so that he was tempted to pay for the room for Jennings, then excuse himself to find another inn. Except. Except that was childish.

Tugging at his collar, Rolf handed the clerk a few llowtxi, then trailed along behind the others as they ascended the stairs. Two flights of stairs. He snorted internally at the irony of calling a set of stairs a *flight*!

"You must be hungry after your long journey." Katilla unlocked the door and stood aside for them to enter a nicely appointed sitting room.

"Ravenous." Jennings set their packs down on a chair in the center of the small room. Scanned a slightly disproportionate painting of a meadow and blinked a few times as if to refocus his eyes. "Are there any good eateries close by?"

"Yes, we have many good restaurants in Civita."

Rolf braced himself for her to rattle off a list as long as his leg, but she just smiled.

"What kind of food are you in the mood for?"

"We prefer surface food," Jennings started to answer.

"Somewhere nearby." Rolf reiterated and glared his friend down. Surface food was more expensive than seafood because it was harder to come by. Especially during the winter months when they closed their island outposts. "Nothing elaborate."

Katilla considered him briefly, then suggested, "I always enjoy the Popina."

"Excellent." Rolf lifted his eyebrows. "How do we get there?" He memorized her directions easily and left her with a slight bow.

"Fine start we're getting off to." Jennings snorted in disgust as they exited The Sequoia.

"I thought you were hungry?" Rolf shifted his historian's bag to a more comfortable spot on his shoulder. "No, I thought you were *ravenous*." His sarcasm didn't even seem to register with Jennings.

"Doesn't mean we couldn't have chatted a bit. Learned some of the local goings-on."

"Seriously?" Rolf pinched the bridge of his nose between two fingers. Though it wasn't a bad idea, it had never occurred to him. "From now on, will you please tell me what you're trying to do? Instead of just leaving me to guess?!"

"I thought all of this came naturally to you royal!?" Jennings threw up his hands. "Listenin' and wheedlin' out secrets, stuff like that?" He stopped in front of Popina, the restaurant Katilla recommended.

"In the first place." Rolf opened the door and waved Jennings ahead of him. "I am not a royal. I'm an historian."

"Your whole family is royals," insisted Jennings, nodding his head yes to the greeter who was holding up two fingers.

"I'll be sure to tell them." Rolf spoke through gritted teeth.

Once they were seated and had ordered, Rolf turned to Jennings again.

"I'm just here to present the council with a copy of the histories. Answer their questions if I can. That's all." He handed payment to the waiter who brought their food.

"Is it?" Jennings shrugged and cut into his hot sandwich. "Right then. Have fun with that."

Ignoring him, Rolf enjoyed the fish stew and hard rolls, washing them down with a cheap persi nectar.

"I'm going to bed," he announced as soon as he'd finished.

"I'll stay on a bit." Jennings lingered over his drink. "Make a few friends."

Rolf shook his head. "Suit yourself."

He yawned his way back to the inn, where he let himself into the room… But he wasn't alone.

"Historian Warner." A thickset man with brown hair looked around from the painting he'd been studying. "Won't you have a seat?" His lips twisted in a wry smile as if he had just noticed that both of the room's chairs were occupied.

Instantly awake, Rolf leapt backwards into the hall, slamming the door behind him. He held it shut as long as he could, then with a single, massive sweep of his wings, achieved the ceiling, where he braced himself. Too tight against the ceiling to tuck his wings, he instead stretched them out flush along the ceiling where he hoped they would go unnoticed from below.

All three men burst into the hallway.

"Where is he?" The brown-haired man

swung his head from one side to the other, scanning the length of the hallway.

"Stupid boy," muttered a blue-haired man.

"Careful, he may be listening," warned a silver-haired man.

"Listening? From where?" The brown-haired man gestured at the empty space all around them. "He's disappeared!"

"You ask at the desk." Seizing control, the blue-haired man pointed to the silver-haired man. "We," he beckoned to the brown-haired man, "will check the hall windows. The fool may have tried to jump."

"From the third floor?" The silver-haired man asked, aghast.

Rolf stayed where he was, toes and fingertips gripping opposite walls. Beads of sweat gathered on his forehead as he continued holding his wings perfectly flat against the ceiling until the men were all out of sight. Dropping lightly to the floor, he tucked his wings and sprinted in through the door they'd clumsily left open.

He left it open as well. They might return at any moment and leaving things exactly as they were might buy him precious seconds. Besides, locking the door was obviously a waste of time, given that they'd gotten in once already.

What should he do? Spotting his and Jennings' bags on the floor, he picked them up.

Retreated to the room's only window. Easing it open, he considered his situation. Their rooms were at the rear of the inn, with minimal room between the building and the cavern wall. Air would get through without trouble, but even as slender as he was, it would be a bit of a squeak.

The sound of steps in the hallway sent him scrambling over the sill and onto the narrow ledge outside. He toed the window mostly shut behind him and stood in the darkness, heart pounding.

"I can't understand it," muttered a deep voice.

"I can."

He leaned closer to the window. Was that Katilla's voice? He scratched her and her family off his mental list of allies.

"I warned you to be careful of him." Her voice was cool, matter of fact.

"You didn't say he'd bolt like a frightened fingerfish."

"He'll go to the council now," asserted another voice quietly. "He'll tell them what he thinks happened and they'll come for us all."

What he thinks happened… Rolf turned the phrase around in his mind. They were waiting for him in his room. What was he supposed to think?

"You said you were going to watch for him," accused the gruff voice of the brown-hair fairy.

"I did." Katilla's voice came again. It sounded much closer than it had before.

Rolf pressed himself against the wall of the building and eyed the distance to the edge of the roof above him. He could make it. There wasn't enough room for him to spread his wings, so he'd have to jump. Once he had ahold of the edge, he'd pull himself up...

"And I thought his friend was going to tell him about us."

Knees bent for the jump, Rolf froze. He only had one friend in Civita.

"Katxa said they were on our side."

Katilla's voice was so close, he half-expected her to... The window swung slowly open, a woman's hand and arm becoming visible.

"Won't you join us?" she asked.

He wiped his hands on his slacks. Even if he held perfectly still, she'd just peek outside and see him there. If he jumped and climbed onto the roof, what would he do next? This was one of the larger tunnels he'd encountered, but it was still too tight to fly in comfortably.

"Who are you talking to?" demanded a deeper voice.

"Me." Rolf made his decision. Swinging back over the windowsill, he landed feet first and faced them.

"How..." The blue-haired man stared at him in shock.

"But he went down the hall," insisted the brown-haired man.

"Did you see me go?" Rolf wanted desperately to pinch himself, to wake up from the nightmare he must be having. "Who are you? And what do you want?"

"Ha. Impudent, aren't you?"

He wasn't sure which of them grumbled that, but it didn't much matter.

"Be quiet." Katilla shut and locked the window. "Rolf, these are some of the galdu leaders in Civita. Koak, Aerulus, and Caneo." She gestured at them as she spoke their names.

Rolf caught her arm when she started to leave. "Where are you going?"

"I must return to the desk." Her blue eyes returned his gaze unblinkingly.

"We only want a few minutes, Historian." Caneo, the silver-haired man stepped forward.

Releasing Katilla, Rolf dropped the bags and moved toward Caneo. Their silver eyes met and for a handful of heartbeats, they just looked at each other.

"Sit down, gentlemen." Rolf smoothed his hair. "I regret there are only two chairs, but then, you're only staying a few minutes."

"I'm not staying even one minute," announced Aerulus belligerently. Koak caught his arm, holding him fast. "He'll never listen to us."

"He might." Koak pushed Aerulus into a

chair. "If we stay long enough to speak our piece."

Clasping his hands behind him, Rolf raised his eyebrows. Belatedly, he realized that Katilla hadn't left. She was standing not more than an arm's length away, watching him closely.

"We've come to speak with the historian who came from the surface," Caneo began slowly, "and is apparently a guest of the Water Fairies."

"Free to come and go as he pleases." Koak folded his arms across his chest.

Aerulus shifted in his chair but didn't say anything.

"If there's a question in there, you'll have to be plainer about it." Rolf had made enough mistakes for one day.

Aerulus smirked. "Are you one of us? Or one of them?"

"Neither." Their response to his declaration was immediate and derogatory, and he ignored it. Walking over to the water pitcher he'd noticed earlier, he poured himself a drink. Sipped it calmly while they simmered down. "I am Rolf Warner, only son of Princess Arabella. Grandson of Prince Nathaniel and nephew to Queen Rebecca of the Silver Fairy Tribe." He'd never expected to have a use for the formal introduction Kuntza made for him at the Cachora council.

"Not advena." Koak frowned at him.

"Not galdu," added Aerulus sourly.

"Not Water Fairy." Caneo rested his chin lightly on his hand. Considered Rolf, from his firmly planted feet to his square shoulders and clear eyes. "Perhaps he will do."

"That depends." Rolf set the empty water glass down and worked hard not to yawn, resulting in a somewhat fierce expression. "Do what?"

"Make them release us." All eyes turned toward Katilla, who had chosen that moment to speak up. "What else?"

Chapter 5

Rolf would've *loved* to sit down. Since there were no chairs available, he leaned against the wall instead.

"I can't make anyone do anything. No. Listen to me." He used the tone that he saved for special disagreements with the adults in his life. Much to his relief, it quieted these adults as well. "I'm a guest of the Water Fairy Tribe. I don't fully understand how or why they do things, and I absolutely do not have authority to dictate to them. Is that understood?"

They nodded grudgingly. All except Katilla, who'd stationed herself against the opposite wall and was watching him silently.

"To further complicate matters, I'm not sure exactly what it is that I'm supposed to do here in Civita." He paused. "Aside from formally presenting some history books to the council, which they will then make available to you."

"*What?*" Aerulus surged to his feet, then sagged back into his chair. "That's unheard of," he scoffed.

"That's not funny," growled Koak from where he stood, massive arms folded across his chest.

Caneo leaned forward, eyes wide with interest. "Are you in earnest, young man?"

"I'm an historian." Rolf drew himself up proudly. "We deal in facts."

The men exchanged meaningful glances.

"Why would they give us books after all this time?" questioned Caneo. "About the surface, of all things. What do they hope to gain by it?"

Rolf opened his hands, palms forward. "All I've been told is that they will allow you access to copies of the histories I brought from the surface."

"Surface books." The rest of Aerulus's belligerence oozed out of him in the two-word squeak.

Caneo put a trembling hand to his forehead and even Koak looked shaken.

"It's really going to happen," Caneo whispered. "They're finally going to free us."

The trio erupted into a vigorous conversation at his words, prompting Rolf to put two fingers in his mouth and whistle shrilly. His mother hated it when he did that.

"Go away," he instructed firmly. "I've told you what I know. I'm exhausted. Now please. Go away."

After a moment of stunned silence, the men closed their mouths, got up, and left.

From the corner of his eye, Rolf saw Katilla move away from the wall. He found her presence comforting somehow. Perhaps because he had three younger sisters? All of them much younger than she was, but still.

He looked at her, intending to smile, and the way she was looking at him made his heart do a backflip and lodge itself awkwardly in his throat. He coughed to clear it.

"Do you need anything?" she asked.

"A few hours of peace and quiet?" He gave her a tired smile while his hands wanted to smooth his hair and his vest and tug at his collar all at the same time. It took a good deal of effort for him to stand still as she stared intently into his eyes.

"I will see that you are not disturbed." She dropped a low curtsy, then saw herself out, closing the hall door gently.

A pleasant, almost flowery scent lingered behind her and he wondered what it was called.

The next yawn that overtook him warned him that he was going to fall asleep on his feet, so he turned and investigated the door closest to him.

Wonder of wonders, it was a bedroom. With a real bed! Not a fishbone bench. Not an overstuffed cot.

The mattress gave beneath him as he crawled under the covers, and he was asleep as soon as his head touched the pillow.

Hours later, he came awake to the sound of someone calling his name.

"Rolf?" Jennings' voice banished the last of his hazy dream. "Time to get up."

"Are you sure?" Rolf lifted one end of his

pillow and put his head under it. Glared at Jennings when the man wrestled the pillow away from him. Opened his mouth to tell Jennings exactly what he thought of the way things were being handled.

"You've got a half dozen Water Fairies out there," Jennings hissed. "Some young, some older, and all of 'em pompous."

Groaning, Rolf scrubbed his fingers through his hair. "Is there any water in here?"

"Some." Jennings jerked a thumb in the direction of the faucet.

Rolf hustled through a spare toilette, then slipped into his second best shirt and trousers. Buttoned his waistcoat and doubled-checked his cuffs.

"Psst." Jennings held up Rolf's boots, which he'd just given a quick going over. His training as Cambrian's valet came in handy sometimes.

"Thanks." Rolf rolled his eyes at himself and stepped into the calf boots. Jennings tried to help him into his jacket at the same time and he shook him off. He needed both hands to get his boots on properly, for goodness sake.

The sitting room was quiet when he entered. Too quiet, as though the seven fairies waiting for him had stopped talking the second he opened his door.

"Welcome to Civita, Historian. Our apologies for disturbing you so early." The oldest fairy in the room, his elegantly coiffed hair a sort of taffy pink, bowed stiffly. "We only just learned of your arrival."

Rolf's eyes darted to the water clock he'd noticed on the mantle the night before. It was eight? *In the morning?* How long had he slept? He clenched his stomach against a fearsome growl. Longer than he'd intended, obviously.

"On the contrary." Rolf returned the bow. "It is I who should apologize, for keeping you waiting." He rather hoped they never found out that he'd gotten there almost a full day before! He'd certainly been right about the pomp that would attend his visit, though. Their clothes looked like they were starched and pressed within an inch of their lives.

"Not at all." The fairy relaxed marginally. "Permit me to present my family." Six pink heads bobbed or bowed as their names were called.

Rolf greeted them all formally, then returned his attention to the man conducting the introductions.

"And I am Yirri, Speaker of the Civita council."

"You do me a great honor, Speaker." Rolf clasped his hands behind his back and smiled even as he wondered why in the seven regions a council speaker would come in person to greet him. A runner could've been sent to summon him to the bilera, as they called their council chambers.

"Now, if your man will gather your things, we can be off."

Rolf accidentally frowned. Smoothed his expression. He'd apologize to Jennings for the speaker's presumption later. Right now there was something more important that he needed to clarify.

"Off?" he echoed. "To where?"

"To my house." Yirri somehow managed to sound gracious and smug at the same time. "It is our pleasure to host you during your stay in Civita."

Rolf hadn't expected that. Not even a little bit. What was he to do?

"I thank you for your generous offer." That seemed like a safe place to start. "However, I have arranged to stay here for the time being." Rolf didn't like the way the speaker's wife narrowed her eyes at him.

"No matter." Yirri waved his hand dismissively. "The innkeeper will refund your fee, I am sure."

Rolf had a sneaking suspicion that Yirri would make the advena...no, the *galdu* innkeeper's life miserable if they didn't do exactly as they were told.

Of course, if he were on the surface, he wouldn't think twice about accepting the hospitality of any of the royal families. This, however, seemed different. On the surface, he was first and foremost an impartial historian. This was an accepted fact. He had no agenda. He wore no strings.

"You place me in a very difficult position," Rolf said at length. "I do not wish to offend the council. Nevertheless, were I to stay in your home, I fear I would lose the good faith of the galdu."

"The galdu?" The skin of Yirri's already pale face tightened perceptibly. "I don't know who you mean." He finished with a sniff.

Everything about the man's posture and tone declared that he was lying and Rolf felt the shock of it down to the soles of his boots. He wasn't a 'royal,' as Jennings called members of the ruling families, but he'd spent far too much time observing verbal fencing matches at his aunt's court to be fooled. And the lie—especially coming from a speaker, a Water Fairy position that demanded honesty!—was enough to provoke him to take a wild chance.

"Then I cannot help you." He sketched a vague bow in their general direction and turned to…what? Retreat into his bedroom?

Just then he made eye contact with an impassive Jennings. Ah, good. They could go for breakfast together. Or lunch, or whatever. Food, that was the main thing.

"Wait."

"Yes?" Reluctantly, Rolf faced them again. To his trained eye, the speaker's inner struggle was clearly visible on the man's face, yet he said nothing to make it easier for the man.

"Will you join us for our midday meal?" The speaker's older daughter dared to break the silence.

Rolf considered. Her mother's compressed lips told him that she didn't approve, probably of his stubbornness or her daughter's speaking up. On the other hand, her father did nothing to withdraw the invitation. Very well. It sounded like an excellent compromise.

"We'd love to." Rolf stepped back with one foot and motioned Jennings forward.

"Well, really." Mrs. Yirri curled her lip. Overrode her husband when he tried to shush her. "No, Yirri, I *refuse* to have a servant eat at my table."

"There are several excellent restaurants nearby," the same daughter—Aurelli?—suggested a bit timidly.

Rolf shot Jennings a warning look when his friend seemed about to recommend the quiet little place where they'd eaten the night before. That would never do for a show such as the speaker had obviously come to make.

"Perhaps that would be best," Yirri ground out.

In the end, the speaker's wife chose an ostentatious restaurant where sparkling crystal glasses waited on a heavy tablecloth and ornate utensils framed mother of pearl plates.

Naturally Yirri asked to be seated in the elevated dining section so they couldn't possibly go unnoticed.

"I'll order for us both," Rolf advised Jennings, wary of the man's sense of humor. 'Hardtack and beans' were hardly likely to be on this menu.

"As you please." Jennings barely refrained from adding a disgustingly deferential 'good sir' to the end of the sentence. Sure he was a servant, but he was as good as any of this lot. If not better. None of them looked like they'd done a day's work in their lives.

When Aurelli paused at her chair and smiled at him, Rolf politely assisted her. He felt a twinge of sadness at the sight of her wings tightly folded against her back and for an instant, wondered what she would think of flying.

As it turned out, Yirri ordered for all of them. Roast shrimp, dabberlock salad, and rolls were served to each place, with lemon crème custard tarts for dessert.

Rolf didn't really enjoy shrimp, but it was food and he was hungry, so he ate politely. Though the conversation around him was stilted at first, he quite enjoyed Yirri's younger children, who were refreshingly artless.

"You like children?" Aurelli fluttered her lashes a tad clumsily, her hazel eyes wide with interest.

Rolf, puzzled but cautious, responded in a carefully neutral tone, "They remind me of my little sisters." After sharing a short story about his sisters, he skillfully redirected her attention to the food and did his best to keep it there.

"Historian." Yirri had regained most of his composure while they ate and was apparently ready to try again. "We have arranged for the formal presentation of your books to take place on the city grandstand. If," he spoke with exaggerated care, "that meets with your approval."

"That should be fine." Rolf washed the last of his shrimp down with a drink of the smooth, slightly tart nectar Yirri had ordered. "When will the presentation take place?"

"This evening." As though satisfied that things had gone his way, Yirri leaned back and sipped from the glass in his hand.

Rolf paused while buttering a fresh roll for himself. Their…difference of opinions hadn't lasted long, yet he doubted he'd be welcome in Civita after the presentation. Which didn't match Mari's expectations at all. Wryly, he reflected that in any event, she could never have anticipated that he would be found by the city's *un*official galdu council first.

"Will I meet with the council before or after the presentation?" he asked innocently.

"The sooner the better, I would think." A statuesque woman with cerise pink hair swept up in an elaborate style appeared at Yirri's elbow.

Rolf came to his feet so quickly that only his mother's training prevented his chair from falling over backward. He had no idea who the woman was; however, her presence clearly annoyed Yirri.

"Aren't you going to introduce me?" Her eyes lit with amusement at Rolf's actions, she raised a feathered fan to cover the lower half of her face.

Jennings cleared his throat, but he needn't have worried. Rolf knew trouble when it winked at him.

Yirri expressed his distaste for the task in his leisurely rise from his chair, including a pause to dab at the corners of his mouth with the linen napkin.

"Lady Izena, please meet Historian Warner." Yirri flapped his napkin in their general directions as he said their names, then promptly reseated himself.

"Charmed," she murmured coyly.

Rolf bravely went halfway around the table to bow over her hand. He didn't recognize the scent she reeked of, but in smaller doses it was probably quite nice.

"My brother, Councilor Quae, is very anxious to meet you." She held onto his hand as she cast a vague glance around the restaurant, perhaps more with the intent of being seen with

Rolf than that of seeing her brother.

"I hope you will be at the presentation." Rolf withdrew his hand discreetly as he gave her a second bow.

"Hmm." She tapped him lightly on the shoulder with her closed fan. Her tone when she answered made it sound as though he'd spoken solely of *her* attendance. "I certainly will." She eased away from the table.

Yirri harrumphed discourteously and waved for their waiter.

Rolf returned to help Aurelli with her chair, then politely offered her his arm as well.

"Aurelli." Mrs. Yirri called her before she could make up her mind and motioned for Aurelli to come stand beside her.

"It was a pleasure to meet you." Rolf graciously yielded the point by lowering his arm. "Thank you for a very fine meal." He included Yirri and his wife in his bow of thanks.

"Be at the grandstand promptly at five," Yirri instructed peremptorily.

"To meet the council?" Rolf smiled pleasantly as he deliberately misinterpreted the admonition. He didn't know who Lady Izena was, but had a hunch that she could make the speaker's life uncomfortable if she learned that there was no council meeting.

Yirri's eyebrows drew in sharply and his cheeks turned a most unpleasant shade of purple.

"Four. At the bilera." Turning on his heel, Yirri marched away, his wife on his arm and their family falling in behind like demure little ducks.

"An hour's not much time to answer their questions." Jennings poured the rest of the nectar into his glass and drank it down.

Rolf looked at the waiter, who'd arrived belatedly. "If you had the opportunity to ask the city council any question, what would it be?"

Jennings choked on the nectar and spluttered, drawing attention from all over the restaurant.

"Sir?" The waiter blinked green eyes at him. "Was there something wrong with the meal?"

"That's a strange question to ask the council." While Rolf understood the man's reluctance to answer what might be a loaded question, he felt he needed to hear the response. Casually, he leaned on the back of his chair, demonstrating that he wasn't going anywhere.

The waiter glanced furtively around the room. Interestingly, Jennings' causing a scene mere moments before had everyone looking everywhere except at their table now. Which was just as well given that Jennings was still mopping up after himself.

"Historian Warner?" the waiter asked softly.

"Yes." Rolf locked eyes with him. Anyone could claim to be him, but he was one of the few surface fairies he'd met during his visit with matching hair and eyes. The mixing of tribes over the years had resulted in a wide variety of hair and eye color combinations, which sometimes still caught Rolf unawares.

"I'd ask why they're so selfish." The waiter's eyes burned like green fire with the indignation of his situation. "Why we have to stay here to protect *them*."

"Thank you." Rolf gave a barely perceptible nod and picked up his own glass. Savored the last swallow.

"What was that about?" Jennings muttered as they left the restaurant. "Are you trying to cause trouble?"

"Hardly." Rolf kept his chin up and shoulders back, the whispers and occasional pointing making it plain that they were being watched. "It's one thing to know what the leaders say, and quite another to know what the followers actually want."

"What do you think I stayed on at the restaurant last night for?" Jennings shook his head. "Lad, you're in trouble. I wanted to tell you when I got in, but you were already sound asleep by then."

"Let me guess." Rolf's lips twitched as he thought of everything he hadn't had a chance to tell Jennings about, either. "Every galdu who knows that there's a surface fairy moving freely about the seven regions would like to know when they can leave." He dearly wished he could tear his hair out, but knew he'd regret it.

"Pretty close." Jennings scratched his chin, impressed.

Rolf nodded. "Meanwhile, the council wants to make it look as though I condone their policy of," he lowered his voice, "detaining surface fairies."

"Looks like it." Jennings strolled along beside him. "What're you gonna do about it?"

"You tell me."

Chapter 6

"How many more shops d'we have to stop at?" grumbled Jennings, not bothering to try to hide what he thought of the fancy clothes on the display racks in this particular shop. So much pink! Hadn't they ever heard of brown or green or blue or black or…or any color but pink?!

"This is the last one," Rolf promised. "It's getting late and I need to change before I meet the council." He hated clothes shopping, too. One of many things he loved about being an historian was that he seldom needed fancy dress. Most of the time he wore plain barkcloth shirts and slacks and everyone thought that was wonderful.

"Good eve, gentlemen." A portly fellow stepped out from behind the drapes at the back of the shop. "May I assist you?" The wisps of brown hair that surrounded his mostly-bald head rose and fell with the motion of his steps as he walked over to them.

"I hope so." Rolf indicated the rack of colored neckcloths. "Do you have any of these in silver?"

"Silver?" The fairy pinched his lower lip between his thumb and forefinger as he studied the white, pink, and black cloths. "I don't get much call for silver."

"We need two," Jennings informed him, hoping to cut their visit short.

"Is that all?" The fellow tsked as he parted his drapes and walked back through them. "I could sell you two apiece and not miss them."

Delighted, Rolf called after him, "We'd also like silver waistbands, if you can spare them."

"How about gloves?"

"I hadn't thought of gloves." Rolf tipped his head to one side.

"You'll want them," the man assured him as he returned, his hands full. "The council here is very formal."

Remembering his first encounter with the council at Cachora, Rolf winced. Could anybody be more formal than that?

"You know why we want 'em?" Jennings squinted at the man.

"All of Civita has heard of you." His back was to them as he rummaged through his stock, but his words reached them easily. "Speaker Yirri is a flashy fellow."

Jennings grunted unhappily.

"Gloves, neckcloths, waistbands." The man announced each item as he set them on a counter. "You really *should* have two apiece, my friends. It would never do to go about with a limp neckcloth or a spotted waistband."

"Makes sense." Jennings dropped the jacket sleeve he'd been pretending to evaluate. "None for me, though. There's only one celebrity betwixt us." He gripped Rolf's shoulder with a grin.

"I would like you to accompany me." Rolf met Jennings' startled gaze directly. "I know you won't enjoy it, but you know more about what's going on with the galdu than I do. I'll need your help to make it through their questions without doing these fairies a disservice."

Jennings rubbed the back of his neck. Grimaced.

"Ah, lad," he sighed. "How'm I supposed to refuse that?"

"You aren't." Rolf patted his arm. "You're a good man." Nodding at the salesman, Rolf inquired, "What else do we need?"

Jennings fumed under his breath all the way to The Sequoia. "You haggle over the price of a room, then pay top prices for these…these rags?" Never mind that he'd found a comfortable pair of boots in the process. His own were wearing out faster than usual because of the all the confounded walking they had to do in these narrow tunnels and… And he'd just agreed to make a spectacle of himself wearing fancy dress.

"Want me to carry the bags for a while?" Rolf offered amiably. The salesman sent them away with their things in paper bags, awful crinkling things. It would irritate anyone to have to carry them, in his opinion.

"No." Jennings huffed. "I've got them."

Katilla must've seen them coming because she was there to open the door for them.

"Been shopping?" She raised her eyebrows and gave them a friendly smile.

"Us?" Jennings snorted. "Not a bit. We're layin' up a food supply for the winter!"

"Don't mind him." Rolf lingered a moment while Jennings stomped off. No doubt Katilla was curious as to what had transpired at their luncheon. She was also his best link to the, um, galdu council members he'd met the night before. "He gets a little upset when he has to wear a knot."

Katilla wrinkled her nose sympathetically. She'd never understood how men could tolerate having cloth wound around their necks just for the sake of an ornamental knot.

"My father's the same way." Widening her eyes meaningfully, she looked past him to the front window alcove. "I've heard he even protested wearing one to his own wedding."

"And I thought Jennings was bad about it." He winked to let her know he'd caught her signal, started for the stairs, then turned as if he'd forgotten something. He now had a clear view of the alcove—yet he almost missed seeing the petit, pink-haired woman sitting in one of the chairs. The same woman that he'd vaguely noticed outside the first shop. And the fourth. Interesting.

"Was there something else?" Katilla came closer, her eyes guarded despite her pretty smile.

"Yes. I'm afraid that with all of my purchases today, I neglected to procure a garment bag." He held up his hands in a helpless gesture. "Is there someone here who would buy one for me, please? I'd do it myself, only I've got an appointment with the council in less than an hour and can't be late."

"We'll have a bag waiting for you in your room when you return." Her smile was positively sunny as she curtsied and hurried off.

Ignoring the woman in the alcove, whom he assumed was a Water Fairy spy, Rolf whistled his way up the stairs and whisked himself through a short bath.

While he'd finished dressing, Rolf told Jennings about last night's unexpected visitors and Jennings told him everything he'd picked up at the restaurant.

"Long story short, the galdu are divided. Some call the seven regions home now." Jennings fussed with the side buckle on his waistband. "I'd say most are content to wait for freedom."

"And others want to fight for it." Rolf gave his hair a final pat and dropped his comb in his toiletry bag. He hadn't forgotten his discussion with Naydie about the truly violent advena who were 'separated' from those they would harm.

Jennings nodded soberly, his neckcloth dangling from his hand, forgotten.

"We'd better hurry." Rolf picked up his own neckcloth.

"Wait." Jennings stopped him as he started to tie it. "You're wearing a Zaila? This is a formal occasion, lad. Shouldn't we at least wear a Rior knot?"

"I doubt they'll know the difference, but…alright." Rolf laughed and shook his head as Jennings' rough, work-worn hands skillfully tied the Rior knot.

"There." Jennings fluffed his knot, inviting Rolf's friendly inspection.

"You made that look so easy." Rolf finished his own more carefully, but he couldn't see a difference between the two knots.

"Try spending a few hundred years tying knots on a windship," Jennings laughed. "This won't be no trick at all."

"Oh! I almost forgot." Picking up his history book, Rolf slipped out the rear window.

"What's that about?" Jennings asked when he came back empty-handed.

"I asked Katilla to have her friends meet us here after the council meeting." Rolf smoothed his waistcoat and jacket.

"And?" Jennings prompted.

"Well." Rolf paused, his hand on the doorknob. "I'm just not sure of them. Or how they might interpret some of my most recent entries."

"Fair point." Jennings locked the door behind them as if he didn't know it had already been breached once.

"Not to mention our elusive friend." Rolf grimaced. He didn't know what the Water Fairy spy was up to, but the Civita council might not look too kindly on his bald rehearsal of the facts, either.

"Right, now don't forget to point her out t'me."

"I doubt they'll use the same one." Still, Rolf kept an eye open as they left through the surprisingly busy lobby and headed down the street. "We'll both have to be on guard."

There was no time to try anything tricky, like splitting up or dodging down unknown alleys, but they strode along quickly, making it difficult for anyone to follow them without maintaining the same pace.

Jennings tarried in the mouth of the medium-sized cavern that housed the Civita bilera, pretending to fuss with his neckcloth. He soon gave Rolf a slight shake of the head and took a seat on the aisle. He'd seen no one suspicious.

"Historian Warner." The speaker indicated that Rolf should stand in the honored place to the right of the council table.

"Thank you, Speaker." Rolf seemed to feel thousands of eyes on him as he moved into position, though he doubted the bilera could hold more than a few hundred fairies, even with two thirds of the cavern given over to graduated seating.

He was a little surprised that they'd decided to open this meeting to the public. He didn't know what the council was up to, but he hesitated to ask the waiter's question in such a varied crowd. There was simply no telling how they would react.

"We understand," one of the junior council members to the speaker's left leaned forward, "that you came here at the behest of the Lady Julene of Kendu."

"That is partly true." Rolf had certainly been astonished to learn that the reclusive Sky Fairy Ambassador to his aunt's court had recent Water Fairy ancestry.

"Only partly?"

"The king and queen of my tribe requested that I represent them." Rolf smiled reassuringly.

"Why?" The querulous question came from someone on the speaker's right, a senior member of the council. "Could they not spare someone of proper age and station?"

Rolf left the question unanswered briefly so the councilor would be sure to hear how ridiculous it sounded.

"Have you of the seven regions discovered an age at which all are wise?" He turned the tables on the man but kept a carefully neutral expression.

"Well spoken!" An older councilor cackled and shook a finger at him.

"Historian Warner." A junior council member looked down his nose at Rolf. "Is it true that hundreds of surface fairies just died in a violent conflict?"

Rolf's chest tightened as he nodded slowly.

"How many hundreds?" The councilor rested his elbows on the table as if they were casually discussing breakfast.

"I do not remember the precise number." He'd never forget those that he'd personally seen die during his time as an observer during the pirate conflict.

"Don't you?" Steepling his fingers, the councilor narrowed his hazel eyes. "Is it recorded in the history books you brought?"

Rolf began to grasp what the council was trying to do—to put the surface world and tribes in as bad a light as possible.

"Births, marriages, and deaths are all a matter of record on the surface," he answered calmly.

Irritation flashed across the councilor's face and he leaned back in his seat.

"Have the surface fairies united?" asked a different councilor, hardly looking up from the quill she was toying with.

"There are still four separate tribes, though

they trade and travel freely amongst themselves." Relieved at the change of subject, Rolf smiled.

"Four separate tribes govern the surface?" She frowned. "What is done in the event that one tribe member violates the laws of another?"

"That depends." Rolf's brain began cramping as he tried to think of where he should even start answering that question.

"There are strict punishments laid out, of course." The councilor tossed her quill aside. "Particularly for the cochetas. The outsiders."

"Outsiders?" Rolf frowned thoughtfully. Another ploy to make the surface seem like a harsh, unwelcoming place? "It is wise to use caution when dealing with an unknown quantity, as I am sure you are aware. However, I know of no law that is written intentionally to favor the members of its own tribe. Of course, there are occasionally unjust judges."

He stopped abruptly when the councilors stiffened. He hadn't meant to imply that *this* council was unjust. Frantically, he tried to think of some way to repair the slight. Seeing Jennings dismayed expression didn't help.

"I understand that a Water Fairy physician has gone to attend the princes of one of these surface tribes." A junior councilor with a nose shaped remarkably like a skewer spoke up.

"Yes." Rolf limited himself to a one-word answer that time.

"Because your prince could no longer walk, if I am informed correctly?" The sentence, though ostensibly a question, came out sounding like an accusation.

Rolf heard the whispers racing through the gallery and actually smiled.

"We are truly grateful that this tribe has seen fit to share its knowledge and skill with us in this case. I know that I look forward to the exchange of information going forward." He gestured slightly with his hands. "I am even hopeful of the future use of fine surface powders and remedies in your hospitals." Whispers rolled through the gallery, causing him to question his decision to voice that last thought.

He endured several more thinly veiled insults disguised as queries, looking to Jennings for guidance as they veered into more controversial topics.

At last the speaker rose and invited those in the gallery to follow them to the grandstand for the presentation. The councilors made quite the procession as they filed out of the bilera in order of seniority, their fine clothes standing out in stark contrast to the sturdy workwear of the galdu.

"Clownfish," Rolf heard someone mutter disparagingly.

Guards lined the tunnels they were passing through, piquing Rolf's curiosity. Had there been some sort of trouble? He imagined a dozen awful things during the long, nearly silent hike. As the tunnel opened up into a massive cavern, he was relieved to find the grandstand intact and an orderly crowd waiting for them.

A crowd so large that the sound of breathing seemed deafening. Had the entire town turned out? The faces faded as he looked further and further out from the carpet they were walking on. There hadn't even been this many fairies at his aunt's wedding and coronation—and she'd happily shared the day with two other brides!

He tried to swallow, but his knot was too tight. He should've prepared a speech. Why hadn't he? A few off-the-cuff remarks would never do.

The speaker preceded the rest of the council onto the platform, where he posed and preened until they were all gathered behind him. Large shelves stood on the sides of the platform like giant bookends.

For some reason, Rolf stopped short of the base of the steps. Putting one foot in front of the other was too much to ask with his knees trembling like this. And it would only get worse as he climbed higher and saw more faces.

He'd never before suffered from attacks of nerves, but right now he felt a deep conviction that he was going to get to the top of the steps and pass out.

"Pssst!"

The overt bid for his attention drew Rolf's gaze around. He made eye contact with Jennings, who shook his wings.

Rolf almost laughed at the absurd idea.

"Historian Warner?" The speaker's voice cut clearly through the rising whispers. "Will you join us?"

Why not? Rocking back on his heels, Rolf spread his wings. There wasn't much room to spare, but he made it. Although he kept most of his mental energy focused on his course and speed, he still flew up higher and faster than he'd intended.

That's what came of a lack of practice. Stifling a sigh, he brought his wings to half-span and dropped lightly to the platform. Did his best to ignore the open-mouthed crowd. Especially the faces he recognized from their visit to his room. Aerulus stood close enough to the grandstand to catch anyone who fell off.

The speaker, thoroughly discomfited by Rolf's brief flight, minced this way and that as though he expected Rolf to land on top of him if he didn't actively prevent it.

"Kindly control yourself," the speaker hissed, smoothing his shirtfront.

"If I hadn't," Rolf was growing tired of neutrality, "I would've most likely hit the ceiling and hurt myself."

Startled, the speaker stared at him.

"Shall we continue with the presentation?" suggested one of the councilors tightly.

"Quite." Still ruffled, Yirri nevertheless produced a wide smile as he turned to the audience. "Civitans! We have gathered today for a momentous occasion!" He paused to acknowledge a polite smattering of applause from the Water Fairies present. "Permit me to introduce our guest, Kaga Warner!"

The galdu portion of the crowd erupted in wild cheers.

Rolf, translating 'kaga' to 'historian,' stepped forward, hands clasped behind his back. In the few heartbeats that he'd hovered above the crowd, he'd seen something unexpected. Instead of green, brown, blue, and silver hair dotting a sea of pink hair, the reverse was true. So, either the majority of the city's Water Fairies were uninterested in today's presentation—or they were vastly outnumbered.

What worried him most was that the guards lining the cavern were all wearing metal armor and carrying razor-sharp suges—metal, whip-like weapons that he had hoped never to see again. Some galdu carried heavy fishbone walking sticks, but it would take years of training to stand against a blindingly fast suge.

As the roar of the crowd intensified, Rolf noticed a satisfied smile on Aerulus' face. He also sensed the councilors shifting closer together while the speaker's wings began to tremble.

Rolf raised his hands high over his head, then slowly lowered them, palms down. He smiled in relief as the crowd quieted.

"Friends! I am Historian Rolf Warner of the Silver Fairy Tribe." Belatedly, he wondered if he should've re-introduced himself like that. "I am honored to have been chosen to present you with copies of recent history books from the surface."

Yirri was abruptly at his elbow and, under the cover of the crowd's ecstatic response, hissed angrily, "To us. You were supposed to present them to *us*."

"I thought I just did." Confused, Rolf turned to face him.

"No, you presented the books to," Yirri's lips curled, "them."

"Then you do not consider yourself to be a Civitan?" Rolf somehow maintained a pleasant smile despite the disgust roiling in his belly. There was no longer any doubt in his mind that this speaker felt he was superior to the galdu.

"Of course I am a Civitan!" Yirri's angry reply echoed in the sudden silence. He paled as he realized everyone could hear whatever he chose to say next.

"In that case, I suggest you smile," Rolf advised softly.

Chapter 7

The speaker smiled unhappily and signaled one of the guards.

"These fine Civitans will have the privilege of borrowing the first books!" announced Yirri.

A line of galdu fairies filed onto the grandstand, their longing eyes fixed on the books. The oldest might easily have been Rolf's grandfather's great-grandfather. The youngest looked to be about the same age as his oldest younger sister.

Rolf hated himself for wondering what the 'fine' fairies had done to earn this reward.

"It's not fair!" shouted a voice from the crowd.

"We all want to read them!" cried another voice.

Rolf instantly held up his hands. "Friends! You will all have the opportunity to read them. As each one is read, it will be passed along to someone else—but the history can be shared!" He was thankful that Jennings had told him about the tradition of holding kontatz, or family gatherings where history was recounted. "None of you are selfish. I know I can count on you to tell your family and your neighbors what you learn."

Yirri's eyes moved back and forth between Rolf and the smiling, nodding crowd.

"What's going on?" he asked through clenched teeth.

Ignoring him, Rolf walked over to the nearest shelf. Finding that it held the more recent books, he moved on to the other shelf.

"What do you think you're doing?" Yirri maintained a smile as he dogged Rolf's steps.

"Helping. Ah, here we are." Ignoring the rolling ladder, Rolf spread his wings and flew up to the top shelf, where he retrieved the history book that started the unit. To the line of waiting fairies, he explained, "This is the very first book of history for the last thousand year period. Each of the books on these shelves contains ten years of combined history from the four surface tribes."

"Only ten years?" one of the waiting fairies ventured to ask.

Rolf grinned as he hefted the book. "I suppose we could think of it as forty years. Though events often overlap between the tribes, the most important occurrences within the tribes are recorded separately."

They nodded their understanding and he offered the book to the nearest galdu fairy.

"Some of the reading is a bit dry, but if you get bored don't give up. Important things happen," he promised her.

"Thank you." She clasped the book to herself like it was the most precious thing she'd ever held.

Rolf's fears about the 'fine' fairies being shams, mere puppets of the Water Fairies, dissipated as he handed out more books until all ten had received a heavy volume.

"Thank you, Historian Warner." The last one smiled and left the grandstand by way of the steps.

"And that concludes the presentation!" announced Yirri. The crowd stayed where it was and his fake smile faded.

"What's wrong?" Rolf asked bluntly. He didn't like one thing about how this was being handled.

"They're not dispersing." The speaker lifted his chin. "I fear it will be up to the guards to clear out the insolent churls."

"I'm sure that won't be necessary." Rolf took down another book. "They'll all leave as soon as we finish…"

"Stop. Put that back." Yirri turned away from the crowd and glared at him. "These books will be distributed at our discretion."

Rolf tasted bile. "This cavern," he gestured at the rock walls and ceiling around them. "This is where the Civita marketplace is held, correct?" It was an educated guess based on the sheer size of the cavern and a few remaining sign poles. The rest of the tents, booths, etc., had been cleared out to accommodate the crowd.

"Yes." Yirri's eyes narrowed. "Why?"

"Because I've never seen a Water Fairy merchant selling their wares at the market." While he had seen a handful of galdu merchants with their own restaurants and shops in permanent locations, the shabby tents and rickety tables of the market were apparently reserved for those not in favor with the Water Fairies. "So what you're proposing to do is leave these shelves here for them to look at but not touch. Is that right?"

"Of course." Yirri puffed out his chest. "Access to these books will be granted only to those advena who earn it. An excellent incentive to behave, I should say."

"No." Rolf hardly recognized his own voice. "How can you be so selfish?" He nearly spat the waiter's question.

"What?" Yirri's glare was practically lethal. "Don't think to challenge me, you impudent…"

Rolf invaded his space, coming nose to nose with the pompous, arrogant man. He'd never wanted to punch anyone this much in his entire life.

"Stay out of my way," he warned, "or I will recommend that your position as speaker be reviewed and the title withdrawn to be given to someone actually qualified for the role."

Speechless at his threat, Yirri stumbled back. "How dare you." But his tone held no conviction.

"A Water Fairy speaker is supposed to be the

the finest the city has to offer." Rolf held his gaze, speaking quietly enough that only the council heard. "Compassionate. Generous. *Honest.*"

The speaker cringed as though each word was the flick of a lash against his bare conscience.

"I have seen no evidence that you are any of these things and I cannot help but wonder how you came to be appointed Speaker of the Civita council."

Rolf's letter of introduction from Mari, forgotten by himself and overlooked by the council, crackled in the pocket of his waistcoat. He suddenly wished he knew what it said. It might give him authority over the entire process of lending the history books. Then again, it might say something like, 'He's here to help, but do what you want.'

Whatever it said, he couldn't stand by and let the council abuse its power.

Brushing past the stunned council members, Rolf walked to the center of the grandstand where he announced, "We require ninety more readers. If your family does not already have access to a history book, please send a representative forward now."

Jennings flew onto the stage and landed beside him. "I don't know what you said to the council," he muttered as he stripped off his jacket, "but the crowd really likes you."

Stretching out his wings, he hung his jacket from the corner of the bookshelf and started lifting down history books for the fairies that were filtering onto the grandstand.

"Marvelous." The last thing Rolf wanted was to exacerbate the divide between the Water Fairies and the galdu. And yet, how could he help doing just that if the councils were going to behave like this?

Discovering a new line of fairies waiting somewhat patiently for their books, Rolf got to work. With Jennings' help, the remaining books were passed out in short order.

As Rolf expected, the crowd dwindled with every volume as the families hurried home to begin studying.

It was only when it came time for him and Jennings to leave, too, that Rolf noticed the council was missing.

"Poor losers, lad." Jennings slung his brand new jacket over one shoulder. "You won the battle and they couldn't stand to stick around and watch."

"Bad choice." Rolf shook his head sadly. "They would've helped unite their city by simply helping us hand out books." Which made him wonder if they wanted to unite the city. And if the other councils felt the same way about the galdu. And…oh, too many things to quickly herd into an orderly list.

On top of all that, he'd just started moving

toward the stairs when Rolf saw someone he'd been watching for.

Clearing his throat, Rolf remarked to Jennings, "If you look casually to your right, you'll see a woman standing alone by the sign post."

"Hmmm. She's pretty." Jennings let his eyes wander past where the woman stood as if he wasn't noticing every detail.

"She's also the one who's been following us."

"Works for the council, I'll bet." Jennings grimaced and hopped to the ground, his wings barely coming unfolded enough to slow his fall.

Chuckling, Rolf followed his example. "Probably."

"What d'you want to do about her?"

"Warn the galdu, though I suspect they already know all about her. It was Katilla who pointed her out to me, after all." Rolf shrugged. "Hungry?"

"Always." Jennings gave him a friendly shoulder bump. "Are we leaving in the morning?"

"I doubt they'll ask us to stay." Running his fingers through his hair, Rolf admitted, "I don't really care what the council thinks of me, but I am worried about how the galdu in Civita will react to the council going forward."

Make them release us. Katilla's words reverberated through his soul. Oh, how he wished he could!

"There was nearly a brawl at the presentation, Jennings." Rolf stopped and looked up at his friend. "I may have helped stop it temporarily, but what happens the next time the galdu and the Water Fairies clash in Civita?"

"You can't worry for them all, Rolf." Jennings touched his arm lightly and resumed walking, though much more slowly. "Did I ever tell you about the fight I nearly had with Prince Cambrian?"

"The fight you…nearly had?" Rolf wasn't sure if he was being kidded or not.

"It's not a long story. Let's get a table and I'll tell you all about it," Jennings promised, starting down a cross tunnel that fed into the dining district.

They passed half a dozen restaurants that had 'closed' signs on their doors before Katilla appeared, coming from the opposite direction.

"Sorry I'm late." Smiling a little too brightly, she took them each by the arm.

"Katilla?" Rolf planted his feet. "Whatever it is that you're late for, we're hungry."

"Too hungry to think straight," agreed Jennings, trying to pry her strong fingers off his arm.

"That's why we're going to my cousin's restaurant."

"We are?" Rolf look back over the way

they'd come. "They're all closed."

"Please come with me," she whispered.

Aloud, she continued cheerfully, "Closed for the special occasion, of course! Tonight you are honored guests."

Rolf looked at Jennings, who tilted his head to one side as if to say, 'As long as there's food.'

"Don't you remember?" Katilla's eyes pled with them.

"We've had a lot on our minds," Rolf pointed out. "But if you were already late…"

"Then we're going to be *really* late," Jennings finished for him. "Let's go."

Katilla chatted about nothing in particular until they were nearly out of restaurants. Then, she stopped at a thick door and yanked on the bell pull vigorously.

Rolf chuckled.

"What?" She looked sharply at him.

"Oh, um. Nothing, I just…"

The door opened and a tall, thick man with brown hair stood in the doorway.

"Katilla! Welcome!" The man hugged her and shook hands with Rolf and Jennings as they entered.

Only after the door was closed and locked did Rolf say, "Jennings, I'd like you to meet Koak, a member of the galdu council." Now he understood Katilla's odd, urgent behavior when she met them.

Koak frowned. "You should not have told

him that.”

“You shouldn’t have trusted me with your faces and names my first night in Civita,” Rolf countered. “You didn’t know anything about me. You still don’t.”

“We knew you were from the surface,” Katilla interjected quickly.

“I could’ve turned all of you in to the council.” Rolf scowled at them.

“No.” Koak’s mouth quirked up at the corners. “We would not have allowed that.”

“How would you have stopped me?” Rolf’s eyes narrowed. “You had us watched.”

“The woman who’s been following us!” Jennings guessed.

“If you mean the lass with pink hair,” Koak all but snickered, “that is not our agent.”

“We know nothing about it,” agreed Katilla when Rolf looked in her direction. “I thought perhaps you might, that is why I showed her to you.”

Frustrated, Rolf rubbed a hand over his face. “Someone told us there would be food here.”

Now Koak really did smile. “The best food in Civita. Come, Mama has cooked all afternoon!”

‘Mama’ turned out to be his wife, and the mother of their eighteen children.

“Sit, sit,” she urged as soon as the introductions were finished. “You will tell us all about the surface while you eat!"

"It would have to be a very long meal," Jennings grinned his agreement.

Rolling his eyes at the not-so-subtle hint, Rolf apologetically warned them, "I don't think it's possible to tell you *everything*." Automatically, he pulled out a chair for Katilla first.

To his surprise, she shook her head and took an apron from a hook on the wall. After a whispered conversation with 'Mama,' the older woman came to sit by her husband while Katilla filled serving bowls for the table.

"We'll be glad to tell you everything we can. But where shall we begin?" Rolf invited questions.

Half a dozen voices answered him, asking about animals, weather, and even surface fashions.

"Children." Koak scooped up the baby and settled her on his knee. "When too many speak at once, nothing gets said."

"Yes, Papa," the children chorused.

"Are we having a kontatz tonight?" asked one of the younger ones.

"Tonight, we look to the future," answered Koak. "Now. We'll start with Mama. Everybody gets to ask one question, alright?" Heads bobbed assent around the table and Koak smiled. "So, Mama. What do you want to know about the surface?"

Rolf and Jennings took turns answering their questions, which allowed them both to enjoy the delicious food.

As the meal progressed from course to course, Rolf felt guilty each time Katilla set a bowl on the table or took one from it. He tried to get up to collect a few bowls for her, but then it was his turn to answer a question.

"The stars? Oh, yes, they are amazing." Knowing that some few of the galdu were permitted to visit the tiny islands that dotted the sea for farming purposes, Rolf asked, "What do you already know about the stars?"

"They're lights in the dark," said one of the younger children.

"They make the shapes of animals," piped up a second child.

"They can tell you where you are," added the original question asker.

"You are all correct." Rolf grinned at them, but his mind was mostly on Katilla, who had paused to clean up a spilled glass and was soothing the embarrassed little one. "In fact, you all know so much that I'm not sure I can tell you any more than that."

"But *how* do they tell you where you are?"

"Ah." Rolf smoothed his hair out of his eyes. He really did need a haircut. "Alright, everyone, close your eyes." They all obeyed, even Mama. "Now, think about your favorite place to visit."

There was a brief eruption of chatter as they started to call out exactly where they were thinking of and Mama shushed them gently.

"Imagine you're standing in the middle of the room. Valus," Rolf addressed the child whose question he was answering, "what do you see in front of you?"

"I see my grandpa's workbench."

"Very good. Now, if you look to your right, what do you see?"

"A door."

"If you were standing with your back to the door, would you still be facing your grandpa's workbench?"

The child giggled. "Of course not. It's to my right now."

"You can all open your eyes." Rolf smiled at them. "If you know the stars, they work just like the things Valus saw in his grandpa's workshop. For example, the night crow flies always in the southern skies; so if he's to your left, you are facing west."

"The night crow flies in the southern skies." Valus lit up. "That rhymes!"

"That's part of why I can remember it!" Rolf winked at him and they all burst out laughing.

Mama sent two of the girls to start cleaning up and Katilla finally joined them at the table.

The questions got sillier as the children got younger, until Jennings had to decide between the dessert they'd just had and his favorite surface dessert.

"Time for bed now." Mama took the baby from Koak and got to her feet. "Come, children, thank our guests and kiss your father goodnight."

Rolf watched, impressed, as the two oldest sons stacked dishes and carried them over to the sink, where they worked with their sisters to finish cleaning up the kitchen. The work was done in no time at all, though they didn't go upstairs like the others.

"Come." Koak rose. "We will talk more in the sitting room."

Maybe Rolf shouldn't have been surprised to find Caneo and Aerulus sharing a comfortable couch when he walked into the next room, but he was. He hadn't expected another informal galdu council meeting so soon.

"Are you all…family?" Jennings gestured at the group at large as he and Rolf seated themselves on individual—and thankfully, padded—fishbone chairs.

"We are part of the same tribal family, yes." Caneo answered with typical Silver Fairy diplomacy.

"And you have more questions for us." Rolf couldn't help sounding weary. He didn't need to see a water clock to know it was getting late.

"We want to know what you told the speaker." Predictably, it was Aerulus who voiced the demand.

"No." Rolf refused to flinch even under the man's disapproving stare. "That was between myself and the speaker." Katilla's slight frown, on the other hand, worried him.

"We need to know," insisted Aerulus. He shifted forward and raised one hand to point at Rolf.

"You made him back down." Koak's steady voice halted the mounting tension. "Knowing how you did that would be very useful to us."

"No." Something Rolf had learned in his historian training was never to explain why he was saying no. Never apologize for it. If he did either of those things, they would try to reason away his concerns, resulting almost inevitably in an argument.

Of course, he was also taught to remove himself from the situation as quickly as possible. And tonight, that wouldn't be easy.

"If that's all you wanted…" Rolf began to stand.

"No, wait." Caneo sighed. "It is true that the information would be useful to us. However, we have other important questions for you."

"Very well." Reluctantly, Rolf lowered himself back into the chair.

Chapter 8

"As you know, we have long desired to return to the surface." Caneo smoothed his shirtfront unnecessarily. "Yet based on what little we have already learned from the history books, things have changed so much we wonder if there would be a place for us."

Rolf smiled at that. "There is no limit to the surface. It stretches as far as the eye can see and beyond. There will always be room for you."

"But will there be a *place* for us?" Koak put a mild stress on the word. "We are no longer of your surface tribes. Where could we live in peace?"

Rolf blew out a slow breath. "There are already small communities that live between and around tribal boundaries and laws."

"Tell us about them, please." Katilla leaned forward, her face alight with interest.

"I don't know very much," Rolf admitted. "Queen Rebecca stumbled on one of them during her investigation into the pirate build-up."

"Stumbled?" Caneo arched his eyebrows.

"They were hidden in the tall grasses down by the edge of the sea. I believe the pirates were using them as sort of a hideout, though they are free of that now."

"How do they live?" Aerulus frowned.

"Why do they have to hide?" Koak's oldest daughter leaned against her father's knee, her pretty face marred by a worried frown.

"They live in an ant hill." Jennings jumped in. "I heard something of them from Prince Cambrian, and it seems like they collect spider silk, barter with small towns nearby, things like that."

"Is it a good living?" Aerulus fidgeted anxiously.

"It's getting better." Meeting the girl's eyes, Rolf tried to answer her question next. "I believe some of the fairies were former pirates themselves. As such, there were few places where they would be welcome."

"And you think we are like them?" Caneo gestured at the small group around him.

"No, I…" Rolf ran his fingers through his hair. "They weren't all former pirates. There were also women and children among them. Of mixed tribal heritage."

"There aren't many mixes on the surface." Jennings turned one hand palm up. "Most times, folks don't get far enough away from their own tribe to marry outside of it."

"Then it's not forbidden." Katilla cocked her head to one side and locked gazes with Rolf. "Marrying between tribes."

"It is definitely *not* forbidden." Rolf spoke firmly. "The new Silver Fairy King is of two tribes himself.”

“I knew they were lying to us.” Caneo nodded and sat up a little straighter as if a weight had come off his shoulders.

“They? The Water Fairies?” Confused, Rolf shook his head. “Why would they lie?”

“To make us easier to handle,” growled Aerulus. “To discourage us from trying to escape.”

“It has been some two hundred years since the last windship fell to the seven regions.” Katilla shrugged. “With no one else to give us information, we know only what they tell us.”

“Yes. I see.” Still, Rolf had trouble believing it. Kuntza. Naydie. Mari. Every Water Fairy he’d met thus far was truthful.

Well. He’d forgotten Civita’s speaker, Yirri. Yirri seemed like exactly the kind of man who’d twist the truth if it made his life easier.

“What else have they told you?” Jennings wanted to know.

They spent hours answering questions about how things were done on the surface, talking until they grew hoarse and the youth could no longer contain their yawns.

“Seems I’d best be getting my youngster’s to bed.” Koak smoothed his daughter’s hair with a fond smile. “Historian. Thank you for your time.”

“My pleasure.” Rolf shook the man’s massive hand. “We thank you and yours for the fine supper.”

Koak and his wife beamed at them as they collected their children and ushered them off to bed.

“Will you be leaving Civita soon?” Caneo asked.

“I expect we will.” Rolf felt his face tighten as he stifled a yawn.

“Yirri will be glad to see the last of us after today, and that’s a fact.” Jennings tugged at his shirt sleeves and tried to remember what he’d warned himself not to forget. He hadn’t brought anything with him, had he?

Aerulus hung back, a sad look on his face.

“Sorry to see us go?” Rolf grinned, thinking about their rocky first meeting.

“I am.” The man smiled, but it didn’t reach his eyes. “As Katilla said, you’re the first breath of fresh air we’ve had in two centuries. I’m…not wishing you were like us, trapped here. I just…I wish I were you. Free to leave.”

Rolf’s heart felt like someone had wrapped their hand around it and was squeezing.

“We’re here until spring. Perhaps I’ll be able to come visit again.”

“*We*’ll come again.” Jennings corrected firmly as he shrugged into his jacket, which he’d finally discovered hanging over the back of his chair.

Rolf turned to say goodbye to Katilla, then stopped. “I guess you’ll be walking with us,” he laughed at himself.

Smiling, she showed them the way out through the corridor where they'd come in.

Caneo and Aerulus must've left by some other way, which Rolf was just as glad not to know details about.

"You two go ahead." Jennings tugged on his knot and unwound it from around his neck. "I'm going to walk a while." Stuffing his neckcloth and his hands into his jacket pockets, he wheeled around and headed off in the opposite direction.

Not sure whether to be concerned or annoyed, Rolf reached up to undo his own knot. Paused.

"Is it alright if I…?" He indicated his neckcloth.

"Of course." Katilla cocked her head to one side. "Why do you ask?"

"Well." Rolf took a hesitant step toward the inn, then another when she joined him. "Some surface girls that I know," he pulled on a loose end of his neckcloth, "would say that it wasn't proper for me to undo the knot in their presence." He pulled harder. *Blast.* He'd gotten the wrong loose end!

"Oh?" She watched him struggle briefly. "Goodness, let me help." Her hands were already working on the tangle he'd accidentally made before she started to blush. "I suppose this is even more improper. Me doing it for you."

Rolf turned his head to one side and cleared his throat. "Other surface girls would say that neckcloths are silly. Given half a chance, they'd be happy to…" He looked down at her and forgot what he was saying.

"Would they?" Katilla came shyly up on her toes to unwrap it for him.

"I…" He caught her by the forearms and gently eased her arms down. "I should probably finish it myself."

They stood there like that for several seconds, holding each other's forearms lightly.

Taking her hand, he tucked it in the crook of his elbow and resumed walking, his free hand making short work of his neckcloth.

"What's your home like?"

"Vitae?" A small smile played along his lips. "Beautiful. All year. Some places turn to mud in the spring or dry up in the summer, but my father has worked hard to…" Without intending to, Rolf spent the entire rest of their walk telling her about the small estate where he'd been born and raised.

"Vitae." Katilla lingered at the foot of the stairs, her blue eyes shining like stars. "It's hard to imagine so much loveliness in one place."

Rolf swallowed hard. Was this how Prince Cambrian felt around Constance? His uncle about his aunt? His parents—about each other? If so, it explained an awful lot. Like why he'd caught Cambrian writing poems about Constance.

"You have a nice place here," he managed at last.

That seemed to bring her back to the present. She looked around at the spacious foyer, the carpeted steps, the tapestries. Sighed.

"It *is* a nice place," she agreed. "I'm a very fortunate fairy."

"Hey you, two. Are you still up?" Jennings came in the front doors, his jacket slung over his shoulder.

"We just got here," defended Rolf lightly.

"Yeah?" Jennings raised an interested eyebrow.

Katilla and Rolf exchanged amused glances.

"Good night, Historian."

Rolf's eyes followed her as she walked across the foyer and disappeared through a door marked 'Employees.'

"Come on, come on." Jennings pushed Rolf up the stairs. "If we do get kicked out of Civita tomorrow, we'll be spending a lot of hours on the train. And you can't sleep on 'em and…"

"Alright, I'm going." Rolf knew Jennings was right. It didn't make walking away from Katilla any easier.

"What's all this?" Jennings pointed at two bags in the middle of their sitting room floor.

"Hmm? Oh, I forgot all about these." Picking them up, Rolf handed one to Jennings. "I asked Katilla to get us some bags for our new

new clothes."

"She's got good taste." Jennings stuck his arm into the bag up to his elbow and nodded. "Plenty of room and separate compartments."

"Speaking of bags." Rolf went to the window and retrieved his history book. "I should probably update this."

"Not now you don't." Jennings was adamant. "Sleep now, update on the train. I'll do the packing in the morning."

Chuckling, Rolf allowed himself to be shooed into his bedroom, where he stayed awake just long to enough to change into pajamas.

He woke earlier than he'd expected the next morning. Dressed and poked his head into the sitting room.

"Nobody waiting to throw us out," he chuckled. "That's a good thing, I guess." The sound of Jennings' peculiar snore came from the other bedroom, so Rolf busied himself with packing, then worked on his history book.

His empty stomach was just getting ready to file a formal complaint when someone knocked on the door to their suite.

"Historian Warner?" Katilla's voice called. "Your breakfast is ready."

Pleasantly surprised, Rolf hurried to open the door. A dozen delicious smells hit him at once, nearly bringing his stomach to its knees.

Katilla stood in the hall beside a cart loaded

with covered dishes.

"Good morning! May I help you with that?" He caught hold of the cart's handle and wheeled it into the room. Realizing his fingers had ink on them again, he quickly picked up the bottle of removal solution and poured a bit onto a rag.

Katilla followed slowly, a peculiar expression on her face. "Do you always do the work of others?" She saw his book on the table behind him and watched in some amazement as he wiped the ink—well, most of it—off his fingers.

"The work of…" He shook his head, most of his attention on the delicious odors emanating from under the various lids. "I don't understand. I just wanted to help."

"It is a surface custom, perhaps?"

"I suppose so?" Dropping the rag onto the table, he concentrated on her question. "If my mother, for example, came into the room carrying a basket of something, anything really, I would be expected to offer to carry it for her."

"But your mother doesn't work for you," countered Katilla.

"No." Rolf rubbed the back of his neck with his hand, perplexed. "No, she doesn't. At least," he brightened, "we don't pay her for her work. All mothers work. And in exchange for their labors, they receive our thanks, our help, and so on."

Katilla raised one eyebrow. "You think of me as family?"

"I think of you as a woman." Rolf felt his face growing red as Katilla smiled and ventured a step nearer to him. "Who is my friend. Because I am a gentleman, I would like to make your life easier when and where it is reasonably possible."

The sound of someone clapping slowly brought both of their heads around.

"Morning." Jennings squinted at them through eyes that were still half-closed with sleep. "Ain't it a tad early to be havin' such deep conversations?"

"I suppose it is," Rolf laughed, grateful for the rescue.

Katilla smiled, too, though her eyes remained quite serious.

"Thank you for bringing this, Katilla." Rolf touched the cart handle.

"I have also brought a message from the council." She held out a stiff envelope that bore a bright pink wax seal.

"I see." Rolf accepted it. "Thank you." He'd opened Mari's letter of introduction earlier when he ran into trouble separating his feelings from the facts he wanted to record about yesterday's presentation. Cautious was probably the best way to describe her language and he didn't believe it would've made a bit of difference in the way Yirri handled things.

"Read that later, lad." Jennings patted his shoulder lightly. "It might ruin your appetite."

"You also have guests waiting for you downstairs." Katilla watched them both curiously.

"Guests?" Rolf set the letter on his history book. "You mean Caneo and the others?"

"No, these are official guests. Water Fairies."

Rolf looked at Jennings, who looked back at him. They shrugged simultaneously. Neither of them had invited anyone up.

"Did they leave a name?" Jennings lifted a lid to sniff at the hot bread beneath it.

"Botere."

Rolf scrubbed a hand across his face. "Has she been waiting long?"

"No, not very." Katilla found it interesting that he knew they were women. Except... "They arrived only about twenty minutes ago."

"They?" Rolf frowned. That's right, Katilla said he had guest*s*. "I…"

"*They* can wait." Jennings set up the folded leaves on either side of the cart and pulled a chair over. "Nobody wants to see me before breakfast and I'm eating right here."

Amused, Rolf lifted a hand, palm up. "There's no point arguing with him where food is concerned," he told Katilla with a wink.

"I can see that." Smiling, she indicated the burl-shaped sconce on the far wall. "Push on that when you're ready to have them sent up. I'll come for the cart at the same time."

"Thank you."

The door had barely closed behind her before Jennings started dishing up.

"So. I'm finally going to get to meet Mari, huh?"

"Looks like it." Rolf sat down and ate, too. He could tell Jennings was hungry because the man didn't bother trying to talk between bites.

"That was a fine meal." Jennings sat back and wiped his mouth with his napkin.

"Finished already?" Rolf teased. "Are you sure you don't want thirds of the pancakes?"

"Nope." Jennings got up and stretched. "You packed?" He jerked a thumb in the direction of Rolf's new traveling bag.

"Mmm, yes." Rolf spread jam on another roll. The jam tasted vaguely familiar, but he hadn't yet placed it.

"How does this work, d'ya suppose?" On his way to his bedroom, Jennings paused to study the wall sconce.

"It probably makes a tiny globe light up at the front desk."

"Really? What for?"

"In Rutegia, they used different colored globes to send simple messages."

Jennings nodded. "Like the flag signals on a windship, I reckon."

"Yes, exactly."

"Huh." Jennings poked the wall sconce and it gave under his finger. "Uh-oh."

"Don't worry about it," Rolf laughed. "It'll be a few minutes before someone can get clear up here from the desk."

"Walking sure is a lot slower than flying," Jennings agreed, flexing his wing muscles ruefully.

Rolf stacked their dishes and wisely tucked away a few things in case he got hungry on the train later. Some hard cheese, a handful of sea grapes, and the last roll all went into the small tin he always carried in his shoulder bag.

He was filling his travel flask from the water pitcher when someone knocked on the door.

"Come in." Hastily, he screwed the lid on the flask and stuffed it in his bag so his hands would be empty.

"Historian." A man Rolf didn't know bowed to him from the doorway. "Katilla sent me for the cart. And," he stepped aside, "to show Miss Botere up."

"*Miss* Botere?" Rolf repeated foolishly.

"Yes." A young woman—no, *the* young woman who'd been following them the day before—entered the room in a swish of soft, expensive skirt. Her pale pink hair was pinned up in a popular style and her gray clothes seemed to bring out her hazel eyes. "I am Miss Imber Botere."

"Oh." Rolf clasped his hands behind his

back to keep from fidgeting. "Your pardon, Miss Botere." He bowed slightly. "I was expecting Lady Mari Botere."

The cart went rattling out of the room just then, briefly precluding conversation. The man bowed once more, then closed the door.

"My grandmother couldn't wait any longer." Imber's keen eyes studied him frankly.

Feeling rather like a specimen being examined under one of their miniature telescopes, Rolf pasted on his best fake smile.

"I'm sorry to hear that." Gesturing at the nearest chair, he asked politely, "Will you sit down?"

"I'm afraid I haven't time. Nor do you."

"I?" Rolf blinked.

Her forehead creased. "You're expected in…" She looked past him and frowned. "I see you haven't read the letter the council sent you."

Rolf had the oddest urge to apologize. He didn't like it. Since her observation technically didn't require a reply, he made none.

"Well?" Her tone sharpened.

"It was nice to meet you, Miss Botere. As you cannot stay—and as I have no plans for leaving as yet—allow me to bid you a pleasant day." Rolf stepped around her to open the door.

"She didn't tell me you were stubborn." Miss Botere tossed her head, realized that having her hair up robbed the gesture of quite a bit of its effect, and stormed silently into the hall.

Rolf closed the door and rested his forehead against it. Stubborn? He wasn't stubborn. At least, he never had been before.

"That one's got a temper," Jennings chuckled.

Squaring his shoulders, Rolf turned to face his friend. "Guess I better read that letter." Striding over to his history book, Rolf picked up the envelope and broke the seal.

"What's it say?" Jennings dropped his bag beside Rolf's.

"I don't believe it." Rolf ran his fingers through his hair, then read aloud, "Due to the success of the presentation in Civita, your presence is requested in Cundi immediately."

"The *success*?" Jennings hooted and slapped his knee. "That's a laugh. You picked the council up and shook 'em hard." He scratched his chin. "I wonder what they would've figured a failure was?"

"Doesn't matter." Rolf read over the letter again. "It's the same effect, isn't it? Success or failure, I'm supposed to leave Civita."

Chapter 9

"Don't take it so hard, lad." Jennings gave up on trying to distract Rolf and addressed the problem directly. "Katilla's a busy lass. She can't just drop what she's doing to come say goodbye."

"I know." Rolf cast a glance over his shoulder as they stepped onto the train platform. Apologized to the man he nearly ran into. "It's just that she's going to be the only thing I miss about Civita."

"Ah, now, does that mean you've already forgotten Mama's tender roast?" Seeing a smidge of a smile on Rolf's face, Jennings recited almost the entire menu. "And that dessert. Mmmmm. You had two helpings."

"You had three," Rolf shot back, smiling grudgingly. Jennings was right, of course. He might make a lot of friends during their stay in the seven regions that he wouldn't be able to keep. He didn't like it, but there was nothing to be done about it.

"So I did." Jennings gave Rolf a friendly shoulder bump and they stopped by a sign to sort out which train to take when. "Beats all how complicated this is." The lines swam before his eyes, snarling themselves like a wayward neckcloth knot, forcing him to look away.

"It's a lot like the ant hill where Aunt Rebecca found the pirate hideaway." Rolf had to stop to uncross his eyes, then gave up and used his finger to plot where they were and where they were going. It wasn't as simple as traveling out to Cordus, the second region. They also had to make their way over to its capital city of Cundi. "I wish the train booklets had larger maps. I could've done this at breakfast." With no sun or stars or any natural landmark to guide them, they were going to have to rely on the posted signs. "I think we go this way?"

"Or you might just listen to me this time."

Rolf spun to face none other than Miss Botere. A rather smug young lady, at the moment.

"Still following us, I see," he gritted out. How had she found them so quickly? In all this…chaos, yet.

"Not this time." Imber smiled thinly. "I had to come here to tell my grandmother that you weren't ready to leave." She waited for him to thank her for her diplomacy, but she was disappointed.

"She's here? At the train station?" Even as he looked around for her, Rolf wasn't sure why he was so surprised. She could've been anywhere in Civita—including behind closed doors with the council.

"She thought you might like to ride with her to Cundi."

"With her?" Rolf gave himself a mental shake. It was bad enough that he didn't know what she meant, he didn't have to let her know. "That's very kind."

"This way, please." Without waiting for further communication, Imber walked away.

"If she held her nose any higher, she'd walk right off the platform without seeing the edge," Jennings muttered. A slight exaggeration, but not by much.

"Maybe she can't help it." Rolf shrugged his shoulder strap into a more comfortable position. "Maybe she thinks she's normal."

"Rolf!" Katilla burst through the crowd and nearly into his arms. "Oh, I was afraid I'd miss you. I'm going to Cundi, too. My father has another inn there and…" Her relieved smile quickly changed to a concerned frown. "But we have to hurry or we'll miss the next train!" Catching his hand, she started pulling him in the opposite direction of Miss Botere.

"Katilla!" His mind caught up with what was happening and he ran around in front of her, blocking her path. "We're not going that way." He started to point toward Miss Botere, then did a double-take when he saw that she'd stopped and was watching them over her shoulder. "Katilla, we've been invited to ride with Mari Botere."

He felt Katilla slowly start to remove her hand from his and changed his grip so she couldn't. "I'm sure she wouldn't mind having one more guest."

Katilla's eyes met his searchingly. "Are you?"

Tired of feeling like he didn't know what anyone was talking about, Rolf answered with a firm, "Yes." And he was. Pretty sure, at any rate. Mari had started this whole thing as far as he was concerned. There would be no good reason for her to object to his bringing Katilla along.

Katilla still hesitated, but allowed him to lead her toward Jennings and Miss Botere.

"Good to see you, lass." Jennings grinned down at Katilla.

"Hello, Jennings." Katilla's gaze darted to the primly dressed young woman ahead of them. Neither of them said a word.

As he made eye contact with Miss Botere, Rolf realized he hadn't let go of Katilla's hand. Well, so what? If he let go, she might do anything. Including disappear into the crowd.

"Are we ready now?" Imber looked into each of their faces and somehow managed to make the question far more annoying than it might've been. Her gaze lingered slightly on Katilla's face.

"Lead on," invited Jennings glibly.

As they headed away from the bustle of the main platform, Rolf noticed how tense Katilla was. He wanted to ask her about it, but sensed that he'd do well to wait until Miss Botere wasn't around. What was wrong between the two women?

Although he had a guess, he hoped he was wrong. Water Fairies and galdu and surface fairies would never get anywhere if they distrusted each other at the first identifying glance.

The fairies and finally the equipment around them thinned out until there was only a single train carriage ahead of them. A peculiarly graceful-looking carriage, with subtle curves and bevels in its structure that softened its appearance and made it more inviting than the box-on-wheels standard carriage.

It even had windows. With lacy curtains not unlike the ones his aunt Gwyneth had chosen for her drawing room at Denboral, her home on the northern edge of the Silver Fairy Tribal lands.

"There you all are." Mari appeared at the top of some steps on one end of the carriage. "I was starting to worry."

"Nothing to worry about," Imber assured her as she climbed the handful of steps.

Rolf automatically waited for Katilla to precede him into the train carriage. She kept a death grip on his hand as she went, which made it a little awkward when they had to pass through the open door.

"I'll send the signal." Imber walked through

a short hallway to a second door. Inside a small room, she used a lightning wire to tap out a signal to the train yard's dispatcher. She always found it interesting to think that the signal traveled along the same cable that would soon provide enough lightning to propel the carriage along its predetermined route.

"Have a seat everyone, please," Mari invited. While they sorted out who was going to sit on which of the colorful, overstuffed chairs, she spun a small wheel on the door they'd entered through, sealing it against accidental opening while the carriage was in motion. "Rolf, will you introduce me to your companions?"

"Lady Damaris Botere, this is my friend from the surface, Elihu Jennings." He paused while Jennings bowed. "And this is our friend from Civita, Katilla Rokoa."

"I'm delighted to meet you both." As Mari took a seat near the window, the faintest of *click clicks* sounded. The scenery outside the window began to slip slowly past them.

"How…are we moving?" Rolf looked around the comfortable compartment, genuinely curious. He'd ridden on the larger trains, with several carriages hooked together and yet to figure it out.

Imber came back into the room and leaned against the far wall, where she pretended to look out the window.

"As you know," Mari began, "we have learned to harness the power of lightning for many purposes. Including moving larger objects such as trains."

He quickly realized that was all she would tell him and nodded despite his disappointment. It was his own fault, really. For a moment, he'd forgotten that Water Fairy law prohibited them from teaching surface fairies about lightning. He knew more than most, having seen inside a lightning chamber during the emergency in Cachora—a huge, smelly cavern with strange metal machines that made and stored lightning.

"I'm sorry my younger cousins, Daniel and Steven, can't see this." He threw the tidbit out as a conversational peace offering. "They absolutely adore anything mechanical."

"Your cousins? How old are they?" As their hostess, Mari exerted herself to engage them all in conversation as best as she could, but it came as no surprise that Katilla resisted her efforts. The young woman wasn't actually being rude, though she did restrict herself to one-word responses wherever possible.

"I should probably ask," Rolf decided it was time to broach the subject, "if you know why I've been directed to report to Cundi."

"I'm afraid I do." Mari sighed. Jennings folded his arms across his chest and she gave him a moment in case he wanted to say something. When he simply continued watching her steadily, she went on. "According to everything I've been told, your presentation yesterday afternoon was a brilliant success."

Rolf looked past Mari to Imber, who continued watching the blank tunnel walls whisk past the window on his right. Imber thought it was a success? He'd never have guessed that from the way she was acting. Of course, Mari probably had a dozen sources. Yes, that made more sense.

"The standing council was disbanded. The other councils in the Muina region are in the process of selecting suitable replacements." Mari disciplined a smile when she saw she'd finally gotten through to Katilla, whose mouth hung slightly open. "This is, of course, not public knowledge as yet."

"Why not?" Katilla leaned forward. "Speaker Yirri abused his power and position for nearly fifty years. Civita will be glad to learn he has been removed!"

"They will be just as glad in two or three days." Mari answered as gently as she dared without sacrificing a crucial point. "Nevertheless. The selection of Water Fairy councils and council members is not the responsibility of the city or the citizens. That belongs to the region."

Katilla sat back with a *humph* and turned to gaze out the window to Rolf's left. Which showed a black tunnel wall just like the one on his right.

"It is not easy," Rolf observed, thinking about all he'd seen during his life as the grandson of a king, "to govern an entire tribe fairly. The wants and needs of the different groups must be weighed and measured against the available resources. Whether those resources be tangible, like food, or intangible, like delegated authority." The present Silver Fairy King was Hugh Lawson, and he had only obtained the crown under the most extraordinary circumstances.

Rolf was so determined not to look at Katilla, lest she mistake his words for a lecture, that he accidentally made eye contact with Imber, who wore what might've been a smile. Before he could decide, or even smile back, she resumed gazing out the window at nothing.

"You are a most unusual young man. And while I'm relieved it all turned out for the best in Civita, we're going to try to do things a bit differently in Cundi." Mari twisted a button on the wall and a short tray popped out. "I rather think you will like Speaker Actare; she's a good woman."

"I'm glad to hear that." Rolf inserted the short sentence into the middle of her thought and held her gaze. He didn't want to cause trouble, but he was learning that he didn't appreciated being dictated to, either. Not in a case like this.

"We'll arrive in less than seven hours." Mari finished pulling the tray—which was actually a canvas-topped table—out between herself and Katilla, then lowered two poles from its base to act as legs.

"Seven hours?" Rolf repeated, startled. "The booklet said it would take at least ten to reach the Cordus region, and another four on a different line before we arrive at Cundi."

"That is perfectly true of the main lines, which have many passengers going to various destinations along the routes," Mari agreed. Smoothing her hand across the top of the table, she traced the outside of a large square drawn on the flat surface. "We will be taking smaller side lines with less traffic and no stops."

"Oh." Rolf didn't know what else to say. The winter tunnels he was used to weren't nearly this complicated.

"If you would like to rest, there are sleeping chambers on either side of the hallway. Food and drink in the cupboards." Mari resumed as if he hadn't interrupted. Tapped the table. "I usually play a game of avius when I'm travelling by myself. However, if anyone would like to play with me, I also have tokens for novem or xakea."

"You play xakea?" Katilla was surprised into asking.

"It's been some time." Mari searched for and produced a small box, which she held up triumphantly. "Shall I set it up?"

Katilla nodded.

Rolf watched with interest as Mari lifted out eighteen round tokens. Nine were smooth and nine were rough. No that wasn't right. He quickly saw that each piece had one smooth side and one rough side. Mari volunteered to play hers rough-side up so quickly that he knew it had some significance outside of the game.

The women took turns moving their pieces along the lines Rolf hadn't noticed on the tabletop. There didn't seem to be any limit as to how far the pieces could move, but only one could be moved per turn. If three or more pieces landed on the same line, vertical or horizontal, they were all turned to match smooth or rough, depending on which held the majority on that line.

In what felt like a matter of minutes, a happily flushed Katilla flipped Mari's last piece over to smooth.

"Very good." Mari arched an eyebrow, not seeming to mind at all that she'd lost. "Shall we go again?"

Mari won the next round and as they set up for a third round, Rolf came to the conclusion that they were going to keep playing. Rubbing the back of his neck, which he'd been craning to get a better view of the game play, Rolf decided he should get to work.

"Historian." Imber, anticipating that Rolf

would grow bored with his role as observer, beckoned for him to join her by the window.

Curious, he did so. Maybe he'd find out what was so interesting about bare rock walls.

"Your friend, Jennings, has already settled himself in one of the sleeping chambers. Do you also wish to rest?"

Rolf chuckled. "I can't seem to sleep on these trains."

"In that case, perhaps you would like to play a game?" She arched delicately shaped pink eyebrows.

Rolf opened his mouth, then slowly closed it. He was supposed to write things in his history book as soon as possible, while his memory was fresh. On the other hand, it would never do to insult one of his hostesses.

"If you think you can teach me." He managed a lop-sided smile.

She blinked. She'd only offered to be polite, but now her lips curved up in the first real smile she'd given him.

"I'm willing to try if you are." Motioning for him to take what had been Jennings' seat, Imber set up a second table on the wall opposite where Mari was playing with Katilla. "We have a few options."

Rolf studied the small flat boxes she offered, then shook his head. "I'm sorry, I don't recognize any of those names."

"Really?" She returned four of the five to the

the tray built into the base of her chair. "I thought you might know this one. We call it tutela." Lifting off the box top, she showed him its contents.

"Yes, I think I recognize the pieces. We call it taldelan." Rolf picked up a tiny silver dragonfly and turned it in his fingers. "This level of detail, though. It's incredible!"

Taking that as his decision to use the silver pieces, she began setting up the bone pieces for herself.

"Wait, that's not right." Rolf stopped her. "The dragonflies fly free along the edges, hunting careless mosquitoes." He placed his pieces as he spoke. "And the frog," he grimaced at the ugly brass token, "guards the prisoners in the middle."

"Really?" Imber examined his side of the board with obvious interest. "I've never played it that way." Her eyes met his. "Won't the frog eat all of the fairies?"

"That's where the strategy comes in," Rolf explained eagerly. "Dragonflies are the natural predators of mosquitoes and…and…" He faltered, then laughed. "Of course, you know all of that."

Imber set her fairy tokens out in a neat row. "I learned something of the surface in my classes, it's true."

Rolf gestured at her side of the board. "You must play it differently here?"

"Yes, we do." Quickly, she set up her pieces. "The first player to get a piece across the board to the opposite side is the winner."

"Hmm." Rolf wished he could turn the board to get a look at it from her side. Since he couldn't, he got up. "May I?"

She leaned back out of his way. "Of course."

He examined the setup with great interest. Only as he started to return to his side of the table did he notice that Katilla was watching them furtively.

"I think I like playing it this way better." He set the frog in the middle and placed two fairies behind it, one silver and one bone. "Working together, we coordinate an attack that drives the mosquitoes into range of the frog and free our friends."

Imber's head tilted slowly to one side. "I don't know how to play it that way." Her long, pink eyelashes fluttered.

Rolf's mind spun, then righted itself. His best friend's older sister had starting behaving sort of like this just before he left Castlemain for Regalis. Except—she saved it for boys that she liked. As in…*liked*.

"It, um. It's not hard. Let's get the board set up and I'll…teach you." He didn't have to look around to know that Katilla was still watching them.

His life had just gotten a lot more complicated.

Chapter 10

As it turned out, Rolf *did* like Cundi's Speaker Actare, who graciously met them at the train yard and walked with them to a nearby café. They hadn't discussed business yet, not as such, but Rolf was beginning to appreciate the leisurely way Water Fairies preferred to do things. Food certainly tasted better when it wasn't mixed with arguments over imports, exports, or fees.

"When I was a very little girl my family's akoa, or eldest fairy, was a wonderful woman of nearly ten thousand years. Whenever she could, she gathered the family and told us stories about the War Between the Tribes." Speaker Petua Actare popped a bite-sized berry tart into her mouth, chewed, and swallowed. "She heard them from her akoa, who heard them from his." She sighed softly. "I would never discourage anyone from learning their history; and yet, I fear there are some among us who still live in those times. Who believe that all surface fairies are wild and brutal. That we should remain separated."

Rolf sensed Katilla straightening in her chair and shot her a stern look. They were guests of the speaker, who had been nothing but kind. An accusatory outburst would be highly inappropriate.

"This is why I am so glad to have your recent history books." The speaker tossed her napkin on the table with some finality. "As well as you and your friends. If we are ever to progress past that mindset, we must see things as they really are. And for that, my stubborn colleagues insist on seeing for themselves."

"Very astute of us, I should think." A tall man, so thin he was almost bony, stared down his nose at the seated group. "Speaker Actare well knows that science is based on evidence."

Rolf watched their body language closely. Despite generations of separation, the basic cues remained the same, thankfully.

"Baron Razoi." Speaker Petua Actare remained where she was, shoulders relaxed and a faint smile on her face. "Why am I not surprised to see you here?"

"Because you know that there are those on the council who value our tribal security." Razoi did his best to puff up his impossibly narrow chest. Directing his attention to Mari, he bowed. "Lady Damaris. I'm delighted to finally meet you."

Mari stiffened, annoyed by his familiarity.

"I have sought to make your acquaintance on many occasions," Razoi continued in serene confidence. "To discuss matters of great tribal importance."

Mari took a sip of her tisane. Raised her napkin and touched it delicately to the corners of her mouth.

"I believe we have a friend in common." Razoi's smile faltered in the face of Mari's continuing silence. "Councilor Fleman."

"You have been misinformed." Mari finally looked him in the eye. "I am not friends with Councilor Fleman, nor do I concur with his radical notions."

"Radical?!" Razoi huffed. "How can you call preserving our way of life a radical notion?" His impassioned query drew the eyes of others in the café to their table.

"Baron Razoi." Rolf got to his feet slowly. "I am Historian Rolf Warner, of the Silver Fairy Tribe."

Razoi sniffed and looked away, as though shocked by Rolf's impudence in interrupting.

"Something I have learned as an historian is that life is ever changing. Sometimes for the better." With an effort, Rolf maintained an even tone.

"Oh, really?" Razoi brought gimlet eyes to bear on the young clod who dared speak to him without his permission. "And what do you know? Our ways serve us well." Thrusting his face nearly into Rolf's, he bit out, "Do you even realize what would happen if awareness of us ever became general among the surface tribes?"

Rolf blinked, taken aback by the sheer vitriol in the man's voice.

"We would be forced to exterminate them."

To his credit, Razoi looked more ill than triumphant as he finished his declaration.

"That will be all." Mari spoke with stark finality, dismissing the baron.

Razoi drew himself up indignantly, then stalked away.

Speaker Actare rose slowly. Heavily. "If you will come with me?" she invited. "We can continue this conversation in my private quarters." She hadn't expected Razoi to make a scene, yet now she saw how it worked to his advantage. "May I hold your arm, young fellow?" She addressed Jennings directly. She liked Rolf all right, but his friend looked sturdier. "My leg is bothering me today."

"It would be my pleasure, Speaker." Jennings offered his arm immediately and squired her carefully from the café. He could tell by the way she leaned on him that this wasn't merely an exercise in social niceties for her. She genuinely needed his support.

Rolf felt Katilla's cool hand slip into his own and gave it a grateful squeeze. Their luggage had been sent ahead to her father's inn and he might've enjoyed their walk to the speaker's home, admiring the droll shop names and cunning displays… But now, distracted by Razzoi's words chasing themselves in endless circles in his mind, he was lucky Katilla was there to keep him from absent-mindedly wandering off.

Speaker Actare led them to a modest, one-story dwelling that sat flush up against the wall of a small cavern. She waved at her neighbors as the group arrived, and paused by her front gate to ask after someone's mother, who was feeling poorly.

"I don't understand," Katilla whispered to him.

"Hmm? What?" Rolf double-checked and confirmed that they were both watching children playing around a highly polished seashell on one side of the speaker's yard.

The older children shrieked as they slid down the curves on the outside of the shell while the younger ones chased each other in and out of it, using small holes bored in its sides as doors.

"The children." Katilla wiped at a stray tear. "Some of them are galdu."

Rolf looked again. She was right. Blue, brown, and green-haired children were happily sharing the space with their pink-haired friends.

"Over there." He nodded toward the far side of the yard, where a handful of girls sat or stood by an oddly-shaped boulder. "Their older siblings?" he guessed. Certainly the girls were not all of the same tribe, either.

"I didn't know it was like this here." Katilla brushed away another tear.

"Oh? Why is that?" Rolf gave her hand a friendly squeeze.

"We don't watch the councilors at their homes." She stopped and bit her lip. Shifted closer and lowered her voice. "We are mostly interested in how they vote."

Rolf smiled at the scene before him. "Maybe you," he assumed she meant the unofficial galdu council, "would benefit from looking more closely at their lives outside of the bilera."

Their hostess passed them on her way inside, prompting him to try to follow her.

"You didn't even notice, did you? About the children?" Katilla hung back. "Is it like this on the surface all the time?"

"Yes." He hesitated, thinking over everything she'd heard him say about the surface. "It's still not a perfect world, Katilla. There are those in every tribe who find reasons to hate others."

She frowned, then nodded. She gave the children a final, longing look before stepping through the door.

"I used to have a big house." Once inside, Petua relinquished Jennings' arm in favor of a cane that she took from a container of them by the door. "But when my second husband died, I knew it was time for something smaller. How much room does one fairy really need?"

Mari frowned thoughtfully and trailed along with the others into a comfortable living room with ample seating.

Petua claimed a plush chair with a footstool for herself. "I hope you'll pardon a slight weakness of mine." She lifted one leg and set her foot on the cushioned stool. "My hip has never been the same since I broke it in an industrial accident four hundred and…" She broke off. Shrugged. "I forget how long ago."

Rolf looked at her more closely, detecting signs of her age that he hadn't noticed before. In the more even lighting of her home, it was easy to see that someone had touched up her hair color, so that the pink was not so faded—except for the new growth, very close to her scalp. Likewise there were her eyes. At the train yard and the café, they were bright and sparkling, full of fun and delight with life in general. Now, though, they looked tired. So very, very tired.

"Tell me, akoa." Rolf lifted a blanket he found on the couch and brought it to her. "How is it that you are still an active council member, wrestling with the problems of this younger generation?"

"So." She nodded permission for him to drape the blanket over her legs and sighed wearily. "You've guessed our secret."

From the corner of his eye, Rolf saw Katilla's puzzled expression.

"I haven't guessed why you tried to keep it a secret." He smiled and tenderly tucked the blanket around her feet to ward off drafts. No wonder she'd reminded him of his grandmother's grandmother. "Did you think I would have some objection to working with a woman of wisdom?"

Petua chuckled softly. "Is that more of your Silver Fairy diplomacy, young man? Trying to make me feel better about my age?"

"It's common sense." Jennings bowed slightly as an apology for interrupting. "In the village where I grew up, we regarded death as a thief that robbed us of our most knowing and experienced folk."

Mari smiled. "We used to hold that same view. Unfortunately, the sands of perspective seem to be shifting for our young ones. They've never known hardship and seek only their own comforts."

"She means they're spoiled." Petua chuckled wryly. "That's one of many reasons we want to free the advena."

Rolf couldn't breathe. *We want to free the…*

Katilla gasped and all eyes turned to her. "You…want to free us?"

Mari exchanged an uneasy look with Petua. "It's not a simple proposition."

"But you *want* to!" Katilla jumped to her feet, then sat down again. Threw her hands up in the air. "You have to tell everyone!"

"First we have to change Water Fairy law." Petua turned one hand palm up. "The terms of our treaty with the surface tribes are explicit."

"If they break the treaty, yes. If *you* break it..." Katilla's voice trailed off when Mari began shaking her head.

"You heard Baron Razoi." Petua sighed. "There are Water Fairies who cling to the treaty and believe that making ourselves known would result in the seven regions being overrun by barbarians from the surface."

Rolf laughed. Ran his fingers through his hair. "May I be excused? I...I think I need to walk a while."

"Yes, of course." Petua indicated her front door. "Folks around here are used to me taking thinking walks."

"Thank you." Rolf bowed to the ladies in the room and let Jennings accompany him out the door. "If you don't mind, I..."

"I won't say a word," Jennings promised.

"I know, but." Rolf shrugged helplessly. "I'm in the middle of this, Jennings. No matter how you look at it, I'm smack dab in the middle. I'll be back before long, so please, just let me take a walk alone."

Jennings scuffed the ground with his boot and nodded silently.

Pivoting, Rolf strode out of Petua's small front yard.

I am Historian Rolf Warner, of the Silver Fairy Tribe. Nephew to the queen, no less. A natural diplomat by heritage. Young, unattached. Naïve.

His lips twisted bitterly. *They want to use me alright. But for what?*

Reaching the cavern wall at the end of the short lane, Rolf reversed course. Walking back the way he'd come, he passed Petua's house and kept going.

The sheer scope of what they wanted to do was staggering. The galdu would need food. Lodging. Employment. Every surface tribe would be stretched to its limit.

On the other hand, it was very nearly spring, a time of plenty. And there was unoccupied land enough. The galdu could be employed in providing for their own needs.

Except… Groaning in exasperation, he let his thoughts come around to where he'd begun. He was an historian. Not an ambassador or even a tribal minister. Or, as Kuntza would say, he wasn't a 'promise maker' for his tribe.

Maybe Katilla was a galdu promise maker. Maybe that was the real reason her father suddenly decided to send her to Cundi. The visit to the inn might just be a ruse. His eyes narrowed. *Inns.* How many inns did Erdi Rokoa, Katilla's father, own? And were they all in region capitals?

"Rolf?" A voice penetrated his musings. "Rolf!"

"What?!" He spun around and Imber ran into him, nearly knocking him over. His hands flew up and his wings spread out to stabilize them.

"Rolf." Imber spoke softly. "We're flying."

"We are?" He looked over her shoulder and saw that they were indeed hovering a few twig lengths in the air. Which explained why his wings—and heart—were beating so hard. "Sorry." He began easing them to the floor.

"No, wait." Imber blushed. "Please." She put her hands on his shoulders and could feel his muscles working. "I've never flown before."

"Never?" He was astounded.

Her head moved from side to side in an irregular, awkward manner. "It's discouraged." Her eyes flicked to his, then down to where her hands now nestled against his chest. "The advena...I mean, the galdu, they used to fly all the time."

"What happened?"

"Our space, it is limited." She lifted a shoulder. "As the population has grown over time, it has become too crowded for flight in our regions."

"That makes sense."

"Also..." She shrank a little. "Flying encouraged discontent."

Rolf expelled a frustrated breath. "So the Water Fairy councils passed a law against it because it made the galdu think of the surface and want to be there."

Imber nodded. "That is right."

"No, Imber. That is wrong." He touched

down lightly and she stepped away from him. "We are fairies. Water Fairies. Surface Fairies. Every tribe. When we stop flying, we lose a part of ourselves."

"Water Fairies haven't flown in eons." She smoothed her blouse and tugged her sleeves down at her wrists.

"Yes, and you see?" Rolf gestured at the… "Where are we?" He turned in a slow circle to examine the cavern where he found himself. "Are these diamonds?" He touched a whitish stone that protruded from the rock wall. There were dozens more in the other walls, the ceiling, and even the floor.

"Yes." She rubbed her arms as if she was suddenly cold. "So strange to find gemstones in a place of death."

That got his attention. "Death?" He looked around the chamber and noticed for the first time how dim it was. "There aren't any lightning globes in here."

She shook her head sadly. "This was once an advena escape tunnel."

"Escape?" He couldn't hide his shock. "From the second region?" The only place they would escape to from there was the ocean above them. The resulting flood would've been catastrophic.

"This was a long time ago and they did not know our regions well."

"What happened?"

"They found a crack in a remote cavern wall and decided to dig." She waved vaguely. "This region was not so full of fairies then. All went well until they opened this chamber and released a pocket of poison gas."

Rolf swallowed hard. "How many were lost?"

"Over a hundred died here."

He squeezed his eyes shut. "What a tragedy."

"For all advena." She shrugged at the cavern in general. "The poison gas dissipated but made many more ill. A dozen laws were created or changed to keep anything remotely like this from happening again."

"I see."

"The tunnel remains as a reminder to all who see it. These diamonds," she shook her head, "will never be mined."

"The diamonds." Rolf set aside what he'd learned about the past and forced himself to think of the future.

Imber watched curiously as he held his hands on either side of the diamond nearest him. "Are diamonds so important?"

"They might be." Rolf winced. "Everything might be important right now, Imber." Walking over to the other wall, Rolf measured another diamond. Then sat on it. "Did you know that surface tribes use diamonds for currency?"

"I have heard that." Imber came over to sit beside him. At a discreet distance, of course. "You are concerned our diamonds would disrupt your financial system?"

"It's a distinct possibility." He put his head in his hands. "These diamonds are the size of boulders."

"And we have many diamond chambers." Imber brought her knees up and rested her feet on a small ledge on the diamond. "But you have so many things that we do not."

"For example?" Rolf wanted to hear what she'd thought of.

"Wood. New stock for our herds of domesticated animals. Surface foods and fabrics." She stopped when Rolf chuckled. "What's so funny?"

"Nothing." He sat up. "Listening to you list off our assets just makes me feel better."

"Though the fate of the galdu lies in the hands of others, there are many like my grandmother and I who are preparing for the day when our tribe is reunited with those on the surface."

"I wish the tribal rulers on the surface knew to prepare."

She cocked her head to one side. "Do you think we would just open the portals and shoo the galdu out?"

"Well no, not exactly."

"You underestimate our dependence on

them."

"I…" He drew his head back and lowered his chin. "How do you mean?"

"I mean they do too much for us. They carve our fishbone, make all of our clothes, cook, clean, and so forth." She began counting on her fingers as she listed things the galdu did in the seven regions. "There is more, much more, than these things," she finished. "Any galdu who choose to remain as husbandmen will become wealthy fairies."

"Yes." Rolf nodded. "I see what you mean." He couldn't help frowning. "Imber, the galdu occupations you've listed. None of them are clerical or in the sciences."

Her shoulders hunched.

He sighed. "Don't tell me. The Water Fairy councils decided that educating galdu might help them find a way to escape."

"I'm afraid so." She brightened. "We do what we can to get around this law, though. Every galdu is taught to read and write. Also math and the geography of the seven regions."

"Science?" Rolf leaned closer when she ducked her head. "Medicine? Law?"

"It was many generations before the councils would even concede that the children of Water Fairies and their galdu spouses would be permitted to study those subjects."

"The children?" Rolf stood up, excited. They needed a way to influence public opinion and this was perfect. "Imber, that's it! The children of these marriages, are there many of them?"

"Hundreds." She wrinkled her nose. "Not all of them are sympathetic to the galdu, unfortunately."

"What? Why not?" His rising hopes began to sink.

"There is no advantage to being galdu," she answered shamefacedly.

"Oh." He sat back down. "You are so right." The more he thought about it, the more he had to agree with her.

"Some would help. If they knew how."

"I think I know how they can help. Anyway, it's worth a try, isn't it?" Determined not to give up so easily, he jumped to his feet and held out his hand. "Of course it is! Come on, we have to tell the others."

"Where are we going?" Wide-eyed, she put her hand in his.

"We're going to…" He paused sheepishly. "I forgot I was lost. Will you take me back to your grandmother and Speaker Actare, please?"

"That's what I came to do in the first place," she laughed. "This way."

Chapter 11

To their credit, Lady Mari and Speaker Petau listened patiently as Rolf explained what he had in mind. There were holes large enough to fly a gyrfalcon-class windship through at first, and they talked for over an hour before Speaker Actare sat back in her chair.

"It's a bold plan," she said quietly.

"It's a dangerous plan." Lady Mari paced the length of the living room twice as she thought. Finally stopping in front of Rolf, she asked, "You want to use the entire crew of the *Wind Sorter*?"

"It seems like the best way." Probably the only way that they were going to be able to get over two million galdu ready to live on the surface in less than three months.

"The best way?" She raised a sardonic eyebrow. "Better than the careful and slow way we've been doing things?" Mari resumed pacing. She'd spent a lifetime building support and opening the minds of her colleagues to the merits of the advena. "We can't just let these windfairies roam the seven regions at will, Rolf. We can't just defy Water Fairy law or ignore the terms of the treaty."

'You already have," he reminded her. Then, in some exasperation he asked, "When you rescued the Sky Fairy windship crew without reporting them, what was your long-term plan? To release them in spring? Trust them not to tell anyone, ever, about your tribe?”

"That's a bad plan," Jennings snorted. All eyes turned to him and he cleared his throat. "Your pardon, ma'am, but s'long as there's a free meal to be had in exchange for a good story, windfairies'll talk.” He spread his hands. "One story might seem like a tall tale. Even a handful of windfairies from the same ship tellin' the same story would go unnoticed for a while. But when over three hundred windfairies what spent their winter camped out on the edges of our known world get to goin', well.” He shrugged as if that was all there was to say on the matter.

Mari squeezed her eyes closed and still looked away from the rest of the group. "I'll arrange an emergency meeting of the high council.”

Petua grinned. "I'll pack my bag.” She started to get up and grimaced in pain. "Any minute now.”

"Allow me, Speaker.” Imber rose with a smile. "Just tell me which things to pack.”

"If you've the need of a pair of strong legs, I'd be happy to oblige.” Jennings took a step closer to the speaker, whose lips twitched.

"Thank you both. I *would* appreciate a lift into the other room, young man.”

Jennings lifted her from the chair as gently as if she were his own akoa and carried her from the room, Imber hurrying along to open doors and pack the bag.

"You'll need more than the permission of your councils." Katilla spoke up after they'd gone. "You'll have to have the cooperation of the galdu."

"I assumed," Mari began, but stopped when Rolf took Katilla's hand.

"I can't think of any reason why they wouldn't cooperate, Katilla. They're being offered everything they want." His eyes searched hers until she lowered her gaze. "What's really wrong?"

"I..." Katilla began blinking rapidly, then pulled her hand from his. "You think you are offering us freedom?"

Surprised, Rolf nodded. "Yes, I do."

Katilla frowned at him. "What kind of freedom will it be if we are still dictated to?"

"You're right." Mari sat down slowly. "However, I assure you that we didn't intend to..."

"Didn't intend to?" Katilla clenched her fists. "I have spent the last hour listening to you all rearrange our lives for us. Teaching us to fly. Discussing how you would prepare us for the cultures and customs on the surface."

Rising, she fixed a baleful glare on Mari. "Worrying about how *your* tribe would get along without us to do your cooking and cleaning for you!"

She whirled to Rolf next. "Not once did any of you suggest *asking* us."

Rolf sat, frozen in place.

"You're forgetting one thing, Katilla." Mari's years of experience allowed her to recover more quickly. "Your voice was heard." She waited until the younger woman looked at her. "You made several excellent suggestions that changed how we planned to do things."

"Katilla." Rolf stood to face her. "Have you ever had a magnificent idea? One that made your mind ache with how much had to be done?" He ran his fingers through his hair. "One that you were almost afraid to tell others about because—what if it fails?"

Katilla's shoulders slumped.

"You know what I'm trying to say." He risked taking her by the shoulders. "You've been forced to stay here for eons. But no part of this plan included Water Fairy guards shoving the galdu out through the portals if they didn't want to go."

"As a matter of fact," Mari inserted when she saw a smile tugging to Katilla's lips, "it's a good thing you were here for all of this." She blew out a breath. "Assuming the Water Fairy high council agrees to this crazy idea, the faster that the galdu can be prepared, the more likely we'll have it all ready by spring."

"We'll have to coordinate with every city in the seven regions." Katilla sounded awed at the thought.

"There's…someone else we should coordinate with. If we only could." Rolf dropped his hands from her shoulders and sank onto his chair. "The royal families for the surface tribes."

Katilla sat with a plop. "It will take time, getting permission from them for us to come up, won't it? And then they'll have to agree on where we can live and…"

"Yes, a great deal of time." He gestured at the front door, mentally including the cavern beyond it. "During any other season, we'd be able to reach them, but now? Every surface fairy spends the winter in underground cities, safe from the deadly weather above. One in a hundred cities has a connecting tunnel to a second city, so that even if we managed to communicate with the royal families, this would still come as a complete shock to their tribes."

Mari hesitated. "It's not *im*possible to contact them. It isn't easy, but..." The sentence trailed off and she shrugged eloquently.

"Another lightning-related secret?" Rolf didn't wait for her to answer. "That's not important. What's important is that we do as much as we can to smooth the way for spring."

"Starting with the high council." Petua remarked from the doorway. She was seated in a mobile chair, with Jennings standing behind her, ready to push the chair to the train yard. "I sent a message while Imber packed for me. Speakers from every regional council will be gathered in Cachora by tomorrow, noon."

"There are those that will oppose this," Mari observed grimly as she got to her feet.

"Good thing Yirri won't be there to cast a vote." Petua shook her head. "He fought tooth and claw against allowing any but full Water Fairies to be trained to swim."

Mari made an undignified face at that reminder.

"You better go." Imber appeared, pulling a wheeled box. "Another reply came after you left." She passed a slip of paper to Petua, who scowled and handed it to Mari.

Rolf would've asked how a message could've possibly been delivered to Imber while she was in the speaker's bedroom, but had a hunch he already knew. As part of their journey to Cachora, Kuntza used a funny metal rod—a lightning wire?—to send a signal to let the Water Fairies know someone was at the surface portal.

"Looks like we have a stop to make in Ten'rae," Mari announced as she read it. "The fourth regional speaker has already lodged an objection and may refuse to attend."

"That would ruin everything!" Katilla protested. "If all the regional speakers are not present, any decision the others make will not stand as law!"

"You're so right, my dear." Petua rubbed her hip and tried to smile. "It might be worse, I suppose."

"How?" Mari practically pounced on the statement.

"How?" Petua chortled. "Don't tell me you've forgotten the debacle of the medical training?"

"Would that I could." Mari winced.

"That was the last time a high council was called, as I recall."

"Right again." Mari's frown deepened. "Calling the council is necessary but hardly an act that will go unnoticed."

"Are you worried the news of the high council will cause trouble?" Rolf was struggling to follow their rapid-fire conversation.

"Yes, exactly." Mari's gaze fastened on Katilla. "Do you know anyone capable of persuading the galdu to wait patiently for official news?"

"We can try." Katilla bit her lip.

"Excellent." Mari accepted the handle of Petua's wheeled box. "We'll get started on this end of things."

"And I'll go see…" Katilla stopped herself. "What can be done to help on our side."

"Good girl." Petua smiled at her.

"The presentation!" Rolf snapped his fingers. "I forgot all about the presentation of the history books!”

“That’s alright,” Mari soothed. “Imber will help you manage Cundi’s council. From here, go to Pida, then Lauga. We’ll send you news as soon as we have any.”

And just like that, they were gone, the door closed firmly behind them. The subsequent silence was deafening.

Rolf wearily wiped a hand over his face.

“If you’re tired, we could nap first,” Imber suggested from where she had remained in the doorway to the speaker’s private rooms.

He managed an unconvincing laugh. “Imber, I know we have to meet with the council.” He absent-mindedly stroked the strap of his historian bag. “But could I have some time to myself first, please?” He completely missed the disappointment that flashed across her face. “I haven’t updated my history book since before I arrived in Civita and so much is happening so quickly that I’m afraid I’ll forget something important.”

As understanding dawned, Imber smiled. “Speaker Actare has a small reading room you can use. I’ll show you.”

Relieved, Rolf hurried after her.

“Oh, this is perfect.” He set his bag on the bare table and pulled the chair out. Breathed a sigh of relief when he saw the cushioned seat. “You’re sure it’s alright?”

“Yes, of course.” She touched his arm. “I’ll

go speak with the council. Hopefully they'll agree to have the presentation tomorrow."

"Wonderful."

She turned back to ask him if he was hungry, but she knew by the way he was meticulously arranging his things on the table that his mind was already far away. The look on his face, too—it sort of reminded her of the way she felt when she was about to make a breakthrough in her lab.

Quietly, she closed the door to the reading room on her way out.

Rolf reviewed his last entry, dipped his quill in ink, and began recording the events of the past few days. Oh, the joy of being undisturbed! He filled two pages with names, dates, and places. Guiltily added brief footnotes of his own thoughts where he might've, as an historian, chosen to interview a primary participant or an eyewitness.

That got confusing quickly and he had to pause to painstakingly scrape away the top layer of the paper where he allowed his personal assessments to creep into the official history.

Imber peeked in when she returned, but he didn't notice. He might've gone on writing until he caught up or fell asleep on his book except that something began to smell very, very good.

Betrayed by his nose, Rolf sighed. Pushing the chair away from the table, he got up and stretched carefully. Allowed his nose to guide him to…the kitchen.

"Hello." Imber's hazel eyes twinkled at him over a small stove where she was working. "I thought you might be hungry." She'd also hoped that leaving the door to the reading room open a bit would be enough draw him out.

He stared, enchanted by this new side. So far she'd shown herself to be intelligent and quick witted. Proud, but not unforgivably or even without cause. Now, wearing a pale green apron, her pink hair pinned mercilessly back, and a dab of something on her cheek, well…

"Is everything alright?" Her brow furrowed and she lifted two pots off the heat while she waited for him to answer.

"I never would've guessed, when we met this morning—" Had it only been that morning? "—that this evening we'd be in a kitchen together."

Something about the way he kept looking at her brought a flush to her cheeks that had nothing to do with exertion. Turning away, she set the pots down on the waiting table.

"You're just in time. Everything's ready."

"It smells amazing."

She hastily removed the apron and smoothed her outfit. Appreciated how he held a chair for her before seating himself.

"We're being dreadfully informal tonight," she apologized, suddenly embarrassed about having to dish up straight from the small cookpots. "I don't know where everything is and…"

"And we should eat before it gets cold." He winked as he spoke.

Emotions that she didn't quite understand raced through her and she looked away, confused. She knew plenty of young men from her own region of Mugan. She'd even tried to be interested a time or two. None of them affected her like this, though.

"To be perfectly honest," Rolf lifted a lid and offered her a scoop of…something soft and kind of gray. "I think doing it this way," he indicated the table setting with the same scoop, "is a great way to cut down on the amount of time spent washing dishes."

Her forehead puckered. Mimicking him, she opened the pot nearest herself and gave him a piece of—no, make that two pieces, please—of baked slimfish.

"I hadn't thought about washing the dishes," she admitted as she filled her glass, then passed him the pitcher of chilled kala nectar.

"Really?"

She shook her head and picked up her fork. "I assumed the speaker's maid would do them."

"I see." He nodded and took a tiny bite of the soft, gray food. "What do you call this?" he asked as he enthusiastically loaded his fork for a second bite.

"That? Strai." She watched in amusement as he attacked the mashed tubers with gusto.

"S-try." He wondered if it was spelled the way it sounded. So many words in Margua resembled the old tongue that he sometimes forgot how language changed over the eons. "This is the first time I've had it."

"Oh?" She stifled a chuckle. She didn't want him to think she was laughing *at* him.

"I've been wondering something." He put his fork aside in an effort to slow down. To match his eating speed to hers. "About the debacle Speaker Actare mentioned."

"The debacle of the medical training," she supplied, wrinkling her nose. "It happened nearly four hundred years ago."

"It must have been pretty bad for her to bring it up," he coaxed when she stopped there.

"Yes, it was bad." Imber folded her arms across her chest. "You remember that I told you the council granted permission for half-Water Fairy children to attend medical schools?" He nodded and she continued. "The decision was set to become public knowledge the week after an important celebration."

He grimaced. "Someone started talking about it early?"

"Worse." Seeing only sincere interest in his eyes, she sighed. "Whomever began spreading the news twisted the truth. Instead of announcing that this was an opportunity for Water Fairy descendants, everyone was told that *any*one who passed the entrance exams could attend."

Rolf swallowed hard, but the lump in his throat wasn't made of stria and refused to go down.

"Some schools were delighted and immediately began administering the examinations to all comers." She pushed her plate away, her appetite gone. "Others set up a hue and cry that rang through the tunnels to the scattered members of the high council. They scrambled to put things right, only…"

"Only it was too late. The tests proved the galdu possessed the ability to learn about your medicine. And the truth about the new law set the seven regions in an uproar." He looked longingly at the food. "Now I'm sorry I asked."

His words were so unexpected that she laughed.

"I mean it," he insisted. "You went to all this effort," he pointed at the pots, "and I've made it so neither of us can finish eating."

"Let's talk about something else. Something fun."

"Fun?" He arched an eyebrow. "What do Water Fairies do for fun?" Seeing her smile dim, he hastily clarified, "Since I arrived in Cachora, all I've done so far is attend council meetings, fight for my life in a lightning chamber, and study history books.”

“And taught me to play your surface game,” she pointed out, feigning affront at his oversight.

“That’s right!” He tapped his forehead with one fingertip. “I think all of these goings on have broken my brain.”

She laughed again and he laughed with her. They continued finding things to laugh about as they finished their delicious meal, including Rolf’s offer to do the dishes.

“Don’t be silly.” Imber waved him away from the sink. “I’m sure the speaker’s maid will be here any minute.”

“Now how could you possibly know when the speaker’s maid is going to arrive?” He stood his ground, which left them in close proximity to each other.

“It’s customary.” Her eyes roved his face, more intrigued than ever by the idea of someone as important as an historian volunteering to do menial work. “We just ate a little early, that’s all.”

“So,” he put his hand on the side of the sink, “all Water Fairies eat at the same time?”

“Most of us do.” She shifted, narrowing the distance between them fractionally.

“Unless you eat out.” He was quickly losing track of what they were discussing. “At a restaurant. Or…outside of the…home.”

His eyes seemed drawn to her lips and he

didn't know what to do about it. But his heart was threatening to beat its way out of his chest if he didn't do something.

They both jumped when someone rapped on the kitchen door.

"I told you the maid would arrive shortly." Imber took a last look at his tempting mouth, then sighed. "I'll let them in."

"No." He held up a hand. "I'll get it."

Stepping around Imber, he walked over to the door and opened it.

"Jennings!" he announced, surprised.

Chapter 12

Rolf sensed Jennings giving him sideways glances all the way to the Camphor, the inn where they were going to be staying while they were in Cundi. Apparently Jennings had gone straight there after escorting Speaker Actare to the train yard, then come after Rolf when he didn't show up on his own.

Tired of waiting for him to ask, Rolf spoke. "Nothing happened."

Jennings cocked an eyebrow at him. "Did you want it to?" He would've understood. Imber was a pretty girl and no denying it.

Rolf shrugged. He wasn't sure of much at that moment, but he knew he didn't want to talk about it. Listening was bad enough.

"None of us makes it through life without collecting our own set of bumps and bruises, lad." Jennings cleared his throat. "Does seem to me, though, that you could chart your course a bit more careful-like." He was about to remind his young friend that they would be heading back to the surface in a few months when Rolf spoke again.

"The only course I'm trying to chart is the one we all discussed earlier today," Rolf responded gruffly.

"Good." Jennings clapped him on the shoulder as if he fully believed that was the end of it. He'd said all he intended to. The lad would have to make up his own mind. "Glad to hear it. So." He rubbed his hands together. "We'll make the presentation tomorrow, answer questions, and head for…"

"Rolf!" a woman's voice called.

"Jennings! Over here!" a man's voice came next.

They looked around when they heard their names. Spotted a blue-haired, blue-eyed couple coming their way.

"Cambrian!" Rolf greeted the prince informally, as requested. "Cap…um, Constance!" Constance had recently retired from her career in the Sky Fairy Fleet as an admiral, but it was all new enough to him that he still thought of her as 'Captain.' Kind of funny that. He'd met her briefly on a military windship last summer, and never expected to see her again. Then they both wound up here on royal assignment to the seven regions.

"Yer Highnesses." Jennings swept a bow to both of them. He technically still worked for Cambrian, though they'd agreed he'd just be in the way on Cambrian and Constance's honeymoon trip through the seven regions. Funny how Water Fairy laws were bent to accommodate the visiting royal couple.

"What are you two doing here?" Constance hugged Rolf lightly, refrained from mentioning that he was getting taller, and laughed at

Jennings' bow. Saluting and expected to be saluted still came semi-naturally to her, especially where former shipmates were concerned.

"You don't know?" Jennings scratched his head.

"Know what?" Cambrian's eyes narrowed.

"You…really haven't heard?" Rolf was puzzled. "I expected the news to travel faster than that. I mean." He shrugged. "No one has told you?"

Constance chuckled as Cambrian answered.

"No, but now's the perfect opportunity for *some*one to tell us." Cambrian wrapped an arm around his wife and winked at their friends.

"We better go inside," Jennings suggested, mindful of the slow foot traffic around them. "We'll be more comfortable."

Cambrian's blue eyes opened wide while Constance's blue eyes narrowed fractionally. Suave wasn't exactly Jennings' style.

"Good idea." Constance smiled. "We can catch up on everything we've missed."

Rolf's shoulders drooped at the prospect of another late night and he trooped inside with the others.

"Sit down, won't you?" Rolf was glad to see there were four chairs in this suite. "It's nice to see you fully recovered, Constance."

"Thank you." She smiled and tried not to think about how she'd gotten the injuries he was referring to. She did alright most of the time, but still had nightmares occasionally. Strangely, Cambrian's nightmares nearly vanished as soon as hers began. "I get the feeling we've missed something important." Constance leaned her elbows on the table and waited for Rolf to explain.

"Y'might say that." Arms folded, Jennings somehow lounged in his straight-backed chair.

"Let's start at the beginning." Rolf put his hands flat on the table. "I was in Rutegia, minding my own business when I got a note from Kuntza." He outlined the events of the last…how many days was it? It was all blurring together, even after finally getting a chance to update his history book.

"She said that." Cambrian raked his fingers through his thick blue hair. "Lady Damaris Botere actually said they're going to free the galdu?"

"She said it wouldn't be easy," Jennings corrected mildly.

"By spring." Cambrian couldn't help that his questions kept coming out as flat statements of fact.

"That was sort of my idea." Rolf grimaced apologetically. "We have the most food in the spring."

"It'll take a *lot* of food." Constance stared at the wall, deep in thought. "Nobody said exactly how many galdu they expect to return to the surface?"

"No." Rolf shook his head. "We all agreed that there would be some who chose to stay, though."

"Hmm." Cambrian bounced his hand lightly on the table.

"That's not a question you can just ask, is it?" Jennings snorted and held an imaginary conversation with himself. "Hey, friend, if the Water Fairies should just up and decide to open the portals, would ya go?"

Cambrian winced. "I shudder to think what would happen if this news got out."

"Nevertheless, it *has* to get out." Rolf sighed. "We chased ideas around for hours earlier today. There's simply no way to get everything ready unless we coordinate with the galdu."

"Which is why Lady Mari called the high council." Constance cocked her head to one side. "I'm still confused as to how she could do that. She's not currently a councilor, is she?"

"Not as far as I know." Cambrian smiled ruefully. "I've been here for weeks and I don't fully understand how the Water Fairy Tribe governs itself." He made a mental note to purse that information more intentionally. It might be perfectly understandable that he'd given Constance most of his attention lately, but as a prince of the Sky Fairy Tribe, it was his duty to get ahead of this new situation if possible.

"Don't blame yourself too much." Constance patted his arm. Told the others, "It turns out that I have quite a few kith down here." They'd be able to help them understand Water Fairy ways now that they had something specific to ask.

"So many that it's hard to keep track of all their names." Cambrian smiled and squeezed the hand she'd left on his arm.

"I'll go see if Katilla's handy." Jennings got to his feet. "She seems to know quite a bit about Water Fairy law."

"Who's Katilla?" Cambrian frowned as the door closed behind Jennings.

"She's was there today when we discussed our plan," Rolf explained.

They chatted while they waited, but Jennings returned without her.

"Her brother says she's out visiting friends, whatever that means." He had a hunch the 'friends' were the local galdu council.

"Well, perhaps we should all retire, then." Rolf gestured at the three bedroom doors. "It would seem that we have a spare room."

"That's very kind of you, Rolf, but Uncle Wynston will be waiting up for us." Constance smiled and rose. "I think he's finally getting used to having us underfoot."

The hallway door opened with such force that it slammed into the inner wall.

"Rolf!" Katilla rushed in, followed by two

men.

"Uncle Wynston?" Constance stared at the taller of the two.

"Katilla, what is it?" Rolf tried not to wince as her fingers dug into his biceps.

"They know! Everyone," her voice dropped to a whisper as she realized there were strangers in the room, "knows."

Cambrian came lithely to his feet and held out his hands, palms forward in the traditional Water Fairy greeting.

"I will speak for them," Wynston told the man beside him.

"Then close the door. There is much to discuss." Striding to the middle of the room, the short, thick man introduced himself. "I am Erdi Rokoa, chief of the galdu."

Rolf kept his face carefully blank. "Katilla, will you take my chair?" He shot Jennings a look and the good man jumped after a glass of water for the pale girl.

"I am Prince Cambrian of the Sky Fairies." Cambrian bowed politely.

"I am Princess Constance of the same tribe." Constance took Cambrian's hand and nodded to her uncle at the same time. "And the eldest daughter of Alexander Kimberlite, first niece of Wynston Kimberlite." She still struggled with some of the Water Fairy ways, but family was central to their lives.

"Well met." Erdi turned to assess Rolf.

"I am Rolf Warner." He silently longed for the day when he was back home, where everyone knew who he was! "Historian of the Silver Fairy Tribe and first nephew," he borrowed the term from Constance, "to our queen."

"Yes." Erdi's gaze dropped briefly to his daughter. "I heard about what you did in Civita."

"I'm Elihu Jennings." Smiling, he handed a glass of water to Katilla. "Nobody important."

Erdi snickered and Rolf could tell the two men liked each other instantly.

"Rolf has told us a great deal this evening," Cambrian offered, hoping it would prompt the others to share their news.

"Aye, and Katilla has told me a great deal," Erdi growled. Spying Rolf giving Katilla a sad look, he bellowed, "D'nae blame her, lad. The word has been out for hours in Cundi and before morning 'twill have spread through the whole of the seven regions."

"What word is that?" Constance knew the value of specifics.

"That…" Erdi paused and tried to draw a breath.

Wynston's massive hand settled on his friend's shoulder. "That the Water Fairies will free us come spring."

"Where did you hear this?" Rolf met their gazes as steadily as he could with his heart beating so hard he could feel his whole body shaking. So much had depended on secrecy.

"From… No, the source of this is best left out of the history books, lad. At least until they're free above ground." Erdi jerked his chin toward the ceiling.

"Unfortunately," Cambrian gestured for Erdi to take a chair, but the man waved it off. "Any desire the Water Fairies may have had to rejoin the surface tribes may cool in the face of this leak."

Erdi's face darkened. "The Water Fairies." He turned in a slow circle and slammed his staff into the floor with enough force to crack the old fishbone. "I was born in the fourth region and have lived my life under their rule. There is nothing you can tell me about their dainty selves."

"Dainty?" Cambrian cocked an eyebrow. Viewing everything from the perspective of a ruling family, he foresaw waves of trouble for generations in the future. Especially if both sides of this situation, the galdu and the Water Fairies, perceived each other with disdain and distrust.

"Erdi, there is nothing dainty about killing trillions of surface fairies." Cambrian let that sink in. "I won't speak in favor of them holding you here against your will, but I will be grateful every day that they found a way to keep the peace that *didn't* involve the decimation of everyone on the surface."

Erdi grumbled something under his breath.

"Can we stop the news from spreading?" Rolf's hopeful question filled the silence.

"I'm afraid not, Rolf." Katilla set her glass down. "The signal originated in Cundi hours ago. By now, too many fairies know for it to be kept quiet."

"We have to get word to Lady Mari." Rolf shoved both hands through his hair. "But how?"

"She will know." Erdi nodded sagely. "That one always knows."

"She'll have to breach the high council's closed doors to warn them," Katilla added.

"It will be permitted." Erdi was supremely confident. "She is a member of the Botere clan of the Mugan region!"

"Rolf." Cambrian turned to him. "You said she thought there might be a way to communicate with the ruling families?"

"That's right." Rolf assumed it had something to do with signals and lightning wires. "And I believe her. The Lady Julene said something before I left Castlemain that made me think she must be in communication with the councils as often as she wishes."

"Very well." Cambrian turned to Erdi. "We need to call a galdu high council."

"Darling, are you sure that's wise?" Constance sent a troubled look in her uncle's direction. "The Water Fairies may know the galdu communicate between the regions, but surely the safety of these galdu councils rests in their anonymity.”

“Yes, that’s true.” Cambrian answered grimly. “It’s a whale of a risk.”

Constance smothered a smile at her husband’s use of the local parlance.

“You must think the reward commensurate.” Wynston leaned on his staff and frowned at Cambrian.

“A chance to get ahead of anything keeping you from the surface? Yes, I absolutely think that’s worth the risk.”

“I’m listening.” Erdi was still scowling over Cambrian’s earlier remarks, but he gestured for him to continue.

“If the galdu hear that the Water Fairy high council is meeting and that they’re going to be freed to return to the surface *before* anyone else does—for example, the city guards and zalduns—” Cambrian cocked an eyebrow and tilted his head to one side briefly, “I can almost guarantee that there will be conflict up to and including violence. However, if they also learn that their own high council is meeting and they are asked to patiently wait for more information, what will happen?”

Erdi scratched his chin. “Odds are they’ll settle and wait, especially if we get the word to them in time.”

“It goes further than preventing violence,

doesn't it Cambrian?" A smile flitted across Wynston's face. "You know that there are those on the Water Fairy council who will use any excuse to block a reuniting with the surface tribes."

"D'you think they'd go so far as to force an excuse?" Jennings asked from where he was leaning against the tall back of Katilla's chair.

"How?" Erdi demanded.

"Well." Jennings rubbed his thumb on his chin thoughtfully. "Seems t'me that the news wasn't supposed to get out at all. Now, in the Fleet, when we want something kept quiet, we do things a special way. Might send a private messenger, might even use code. Point is, the message gets where it's going and nowheres else."

Erdi and Wynston gave each other a long look.

"Yes, there are such measures taken here, also," Wynston admitted at last.

"That's how you knew it was an important message," Rolf deduced suddenly. "The ordinary messages get handled one way, so if anything is treated differently, you notice and make a point of getting ahold of it."

Erdi grimaced, then smiled. "You're a canny one, lad."

Constance observed Erdi wink at Katilla, who promptly blushed. She flicked a glance at Rolf, who didn't have a clue.

"And if they had any inkling this was going on," Constance inserted quietly, "this would be the perfect opportunity for them to use it against you."

"Absolutely." Cambrian was surprised that he hadn't been the one to think of it, especially after all of his years as a special investigator for the crown.

"You make a good argument, Cambrian." Wynston winked at Constance, please that she'd made such a good match. "Unfortunately, even if we could convince the galdu to convene a high council, as you call it, there isn't a way to get them all together."

"He's right." Erdi pulled a piece of paper out of his belt pouch and waved it at them. "My travel permit. I can go visit any of my inns whenever I want. So long as I tell the city guard where I'm going and when. And of course, I have to check in when I arrive at the next city."

"That's only when travelling out toward the seventh region, though." Katilla knew because, as a member of the family business, she had an identical pass. "We can travel in, toward the center, without all of that."

"Aye, but since we're only in the second region, what's to be done?" Erdi pointed out, not unkindly. "No, by the time we got permission to go get them and permission to come back with them, it'd all be over but the shouting."

"You're not even counting travel time."

Wynston shook his head. "And the haggling as to which region we should meet in."

"Can't we send a message to them?" Cambrian frowned, still puzzling through it all. "They could at least try to meet, all of them in the capital of the fourth region, since it's the most centrally located."

"I admire your gumption, but again, it's impossible," Erdi answered a bit glumly. "Only Water Fairies can send signals."

"If I understand you correctly," Rolf interrupted, "we need to persuade the galdu councilors to risk meeting openly and find a way to get them all to the capital city of the fourth region."

"Sounds t'me like you have an idea." Jennings squinted at his young friend.

"I might." Rolf wasn't ready to volunteer Imber to the group and hoped Jennings wouldn't do it for him. "I'm not promising anything."

"But you *do* have an idea." Constance smiled, reflecting that Rolf had a rare knack for getting himself into troublesome situations. And out of them.

"Can we spare an hour?" he countered.

"Imber." Katilla stood up and faced him. "You think she'll help *us*?"

Rolf assumed an impassive expression.

"And what if she turns us all in as conspirators?" Katilla nearly clapped a hand over her mouth. The label of 'conspirator' was a permanent shadow on a galdu's life. Constantly watched by the city guards, they were among the first to be questioned in the event of trouble. Any kind of trouble.

"Rolf." Constance walked over to him and took him by the shoulders. "You said Imber was Mari's granddaughter." She studied him closely.

"That's right."

"Is there any way your plan would work without her help?"

He hesitated. Could they possibly steal the private carriage? No, that wouldn't work. None of them had the faintest idea of how to operate it. At any rate, Mari had taken it with her to Triens. Imber would have to call for it or another one just like it.

"I don't think so, no."

"I believe him." Satisfied with what she saw in his face and eyes, Constance squeezed his shoulders and let him go.

"So do I." Cambrian was quick to agree.

"Take your hour." Erdi looked up from where he'd been conversing quietly with Katilla. "We'll need the time to prepare. Only mark carefully how much you tell her." He held up a warning finger.

"I'll be discreet." Rolf frowned faintly at Jennings, who seemed about to offer to accompany him, and stepped out into the hallway.

Chapter 13

Imber sat, cross-legged, just inside the seashell in the speaker's front yard. The area children were all fast asleep by now, but somehow she couldn't seem to manage. She'd tried blaming her restlessness on the borrowed bed. She'd tried reciting the elements in reverse order. Nothing helped tonight.

Tired of being alone in a strange house, she'd stolen softly across the yard and hidden herself in the seashell to think.

It was all the excitement, of course. Being a part, even a teeny-tiny part, of helping to free the detained galdu from her tribe was very exciting. Oh, how everything would change! The seven regions would feel very empty after they opened the surface portals. She could hardly imagine it. Of course, some of the galdu might choose to stay, but millions of them would pack up their things and leave.

Leave. He'll be leaving soon.

Sternly, she redirected her thoughts from the silver-eyed historian.

Looping her pink braid over her shoulder, she leaned back and tried to picture the surface. Not the wild islands of her sea, but the broad forests, rolling meadows, and tall, tall mountains she'd heard about.

Maybe she would visit the surface next year.

As a scientist, it would literally be a new world for her to explore. Hundreds of plant species for her examine.

Her lips twitched as she thought of the cautious way Rolf tasted the strai at supper. He seemed to like it, which made her very happy.

Putting her head in her hands, she brought her thoughts once more to the *real* reason she was wide awake.

Studying the surface flora might take the rest of her lifetime! Recording medicinal properties… Mmmm, the surface doctors had surely done that by now, but she could study their work with fresh eyes and perhaps even make improvements given enough time.

Yes, she would go to the surface. She'd visit the Plant Fairy Tribe and… At least, she'd *like* to visit the Plant Fairy Tribe. She hoped they'd allow it. The thought of asking for permission after a lifetime of going where and when she chose made her stomach tighten.

Oh, how everything would change.

Drawing circles with her fingertip on the smooth nacre wall beside her, she pondered the matter. Perhaps she should start with the so-called diplomats of the surface tribes, the Silver Fairies. They would almost certainly welcome visitors. And, if she happened to accidentally run into a certain young man…who hadn't kissed her when she wanted him to…

Sighing, she leaned against the wall. She

might as well admit it. She couldn't sleep because she couldn't stop thinking of Rolf. Pity she hadn't been nicer to him at first. Did she really expect a cocheta like him to know that a letter from a regional council was to be opened immediately?

But no, she'd breezed into his room at the inn and jumped to conclusions. Then there was the way the girl from the inn—Katilla, she reminded herself—showed up at the train yard.

Imber definitely hadn't expected that. Or Rolf's simple confidence in standing up to her. She'd admired his directness with her grandmother, too. His patience as he taught her how to play tald…um. Tal…

Try as she would, she couldn't recall the strange name he'd used. She'd have to remember to ask him the next time she saw him. Whatever he'd called it, she'd had much more fun playing the game with both sides working as a team to rescue their lost tribesfairies than she'd ever had playing it the other way.

"Imber?"

She gave a small scream and jerked her feet up out of sight from the outside.

Rolf jumped nearly a twig's length into the air and hovered, wings extended and flapping as if they had a mind of their own.

As the air stirred around her, Imber recognized what was happening. It was exactly like earlier when Rolf flew in the cavern.

"Rolf?" she called. "Is that you?"

He put a hand to his erratically beating heart and landed lightly.

"Imber?" Ducking down, he crawled in through the child-sized door and sat beside her. "You nearly stopped my heart! Why did you scream?" It was hard for him to stay mad at her when she smelled sweet and looked like springtime. She'd changed into something soft and a little frilly. Her hair was down in a braid, too, much more like what he was used to.

"Because you scared me half to death," she retorted automatically.

"I guess I did." Rolf's lips twitched as he reached behind himself to straighten the back of his jacket. The wing slits were tailored perfectly to him when he left Castlemain, but that was weeks ago and he was still growing. "Sorry about that."

"I'm sorry I screamed," she returned quickly.

"No, you had good reason." He looked around the interior of the seashell in wonder. The various holes cut in it to let the children play allowed some of the light to seep in from the lightning globes outside. "This is amazing."

"Haven't you ever been inside a seashell before?"

"First time." He stroked the smooth, pearl-like surface underneath him.

"I suppose there are lots of things you've never done." The thought escaped before she'd finished evaluating it. He didn't seem to mind.

"That makes sense," he agreed with a smile. "And probably the reverse is true."

"For example?" She wrapped her arms around her knees.

Even in the dim light, he could see the interest on her face, hear it in her voice. The intensity of it surprised him. Unfortunately, he hadn't come here to chat with a friend.

"I'm sorry, Imber, I want to talk with you about the surface or life in the seven regions," *or just about anything you like,* "but I don't have much time and we need your help."

Disappointed, she schooled her voice and asked calmly, "We?" One of the benefits of being born into the Botere family was that she'd learned young how to present only the side she wanted to have seen. Most of the time.

"I should start at the beginning." As quickly as he could, he told her everything he'd rehearsed on the long walk over. There were some pretty large, gaping holes, and he could tell that troubled her.

She frowned when he dodged some of her questions, but thought she understood why he did. Being caretaker of someone else's secrets was never easy.

"You want me to help you smuggle seven galdu leaders into Triens," she summarized at last.

"Yes. Ummm…" Embarrassed, he rubbed

the back of his neck. "Please."

Sighing, she pinched the bridge of her nose and tried to think if it could even be done.

"It will take too long for us to gather them in Triens. We should collect them and head straight for Cachora."

"Are you sure?" She dropped her hand from her face and looked at him, causing him to raise his hands in surrender. "We thought that bringing them to the fourth region would save time."

"Since we only have one carriage, I'm afraid not." A thought occurred to her as she stood up and she added, "Taking them to Cachora will also lend credibility to their mission. They'll be in the same city and meeting at the same time as the Water Fairy high council."

He whistled softly and followed her through the one adult-sized door in the seashell. Not for the first time he thought how strange it was that the lightning globes stayed on all day. They were dimmed now, as if to mimic stars without remotely resembling them.

On the other hand, with Imber to look at, who needed stars? Good grief, he was starting to sound like Cambrian, the poet-prince.

He cleared his throat and threw out the first question that sprang to mind.

"Is there a chance, however remote, that the Water Fairy high council would recognize the galdu council? Meet with them, face to face?"

"Rolf, you mustn't even think that," she half-scolded, startled at his brazenness. "If you think it, you might say it and then where would we be?" In even more trouble, that was where. The high council would not take a suggestion like that lightly.

"That sounds like something my grandmother would say." He chuckled, back on safe ground with himself.

Not sure how to take that, she reached out to give him a little push. Much to her surprise, he captured her hand—and refused to let it go when she tugged on it.

"Mine," he announced.

"Rolf, don't be silly." Her stomach did a little flip when he moved closer.

"Me? Me, silly?" He let go of her hand but didn't retreat. "I would never."

"Oh." That was it? That was all she could think to say? "I…better send the signal for my carriage." She thought she saw a flash of emotion in his eyes, but it was too dark to be sure. Or at last, that's what she told herself as she hurried inside to change out of her pajamas.

Rolf smothered his disappointment when she reappeared wearing a plain plum-colored shirt and dark blue straight-line skirt. A no-nonsense bag hung over one shoulder. It might be just the outfit for committing treason, but he doubted he'd be teasing her while she wore it.

"The carriage is on its way," she announced.

"Now I need to know where we're going to pick up whom."

"Imber." He stopped her at the front door. "There's some concern that you'll turn them in as conspirators." He braced himself for an angry response.

Her heart twisted painfully in her chest and she nodded.

"Very wise of them. Under the circumstances, I mean." And yet, she'd do nothing of the kind. How could she expect them to believe that?

Not knowing what else to do, she placed her hand on his chest, where she could feel his pounding heart, and solemnly pledged, "Whatever fate befalls the galdu council, I will face with them."

"As will I." He took her hand and sealed his promise with a kiss pressed to her palm, the way he'd seen his father kiss his mother's hand. Imber's face flamed in response and he smiled, suddenly feeling quite roguish. "We better get going."

Not trusting herself to speak, she simply nodded and stepped briskly into the night. Feeling the air stir about her, she looked up and was startled to find Rolf hovering a few feet away from her.

"Come on." He stretched his hand out to her.

Her heart leapt with such force that she

thought she could hear her teeth rattle.

Why not? her head cautiously agreed.

She spread her wings. Water Fairy doctors recommended a basic wing workout that significantly reduced back pain, so it wasn't as if she had no muscle tone whatsoever.

"Good," he approved, dropping down to almost her level. "Now this sounds silly, but it's imperative that you remember to breathe."

"Very funny." She rolled her eyes at him.

"Laugh all you like." His hand closed gently about hers. "You'll see what I mean soon enough."

Since he had more experience and a tad more control, he led the way, careful to keep his near wing from striking her as their wings beat the air.

As slowly as they went, she felt a difference in the drafts in the empty tunnels they traversed. Tried to follow him through a simple spin in a small cavern and laughed when he had to catch her because she lost track of which way was up.

Then they swooped into a connecting tunnel and the tip of her wing grazed a wall. Her smile died abruptly. No wonder the galdu wanted to go back to the surface. Her home had never before seemed so narrow, so limiting.

She gamely stayed with him for about half the distance to the inn before his warning caught up with her.

Sensing her distress, he pulled up abruptly

and drew her to a standing position beside him.

"So…hard," she gasped, "to synchronize."

"Easy." He cupped her face in his hands. "Slowly as you can. Actually fill your lungs. Good." He began breathing with her, pacing her. "You did fabulously, you know."

She tried to laugh, but her heart was racing for a whole new reason now. If he lowered his hands even a little, he would've been able to feel her pulse pounding in her neck vein.

"C'mon." He tucked her hand through his arm. "We'll walk the rest of the way, alright?"

Nodding, she fell in beside him, liking the proximity.

"Well?" He squeezed her hand gently. "What did you think?"

"About flying?" Her voice trembled and she tried to laugh. "It's absolutely exhilarating."

"You'll love flying on the surface," he promised, carried away by the experience. "It's completely different. The horizon stretches ahead of you for days. The sun is warm on your wings and the air is cool from the earth below. And if you get very high at all, the breezes can be positively mischievous."

"I'm not sure I like the sound of that last," she admitted. The rest of it sounded all too wonderful. Especially if he was offering to show it to her. Much to her surprise, he shifted to put an arm around her shoulders as though to protect her from something.

"It can be dangerous, I won't lie." His own aunt had died in a freak flying accident when she was just about his age. That was something he'd never be able to forget. "Don't worry. We'll take lessons together and have a wonderful time."

"Lessons?" She stared up at him. "Do you mean that you didn't learn to fly the same way you learned to walk?"

He laughed. "Of course I did. Someone taught me to walk, and now that my wings have finished growing, I'm being taught how to fly."

They continued discussing the subject as they walked until he'd taught her what little he knew.

"You mean birds *eat* fairies?" She was aghast.

"I said birds will eat fairies *if*," he stressed the uncertainty, "the fairy isn't being watchful." She shivered and he tightened his arm around her shoulders. "I'm sorry, that's not a very nice thing to talk about, is it?"

"No," she agreed, then sighed. "Yet I should've expected it. Our waters are just as full of predators as your skies."

He discreetly lowered his arm when the Camphor came into view and she missed its warmth immediately. The lobby was quiet when they entered, the clerk dozing peacefully at his post behind the big desk.

"There you two are!" Constance got up from

the table the instant they walked into the sitting room.

"Constance?" Rolf swept the room with his gaze, but no one else was there.

"The others got nervous." Constance caught up her jacket and slipped it on. "I agreed to wait here while Cambrian went with them to…" She paused and raised an inquisitive eyebrow at Imber.

"Miss Imber Botere," Rolf leapt into the gap, "I'd like you to meet my extraordinary friend, Princess Constance Bijou, lately of the Sky Fairy Fleet."

Constance inclined her head slightly in acknowledgement of the introduction and Imber mimicked the motion.

"I saw you at the bilera in Cachora," Imber confessed. She hadn't said a word about that to Rolf and now she wondered if she should have. "You are a credit to your tribe."

"Thank you." Constance finished buttoning her jacket and asked bluntly, "Does that mean you will be helping us?"

"I consider this an opportunity to help all of the tribes." Imber met her gaze confidently. "My carriage and I are at your disposal."

"Excellent." Constance picked up Rolf's historian's bag and handed it to him. "Jennings asked me to look after this while you were gone."

"Thank you." He slipped the strap over his shoulder and took Imber by the hand. "After you, Your Highness."

Constance grimaced. "Let's keep the titles to a minimum, shall we? We'll attract less attention that way." It had taken her nearly four weeks to get past the popular concept that she was somehow a hero of the seven regions.

She quizzed him about his family and Imber about hers as they casually made their way to where Cambrian and the others were. Like most Water Fairy cities, Cundi was never fully asleep, so they nodded politely to the occasional passing fairy and continued calmly on their way.

"Is there a reason we're walking in circles?" Imber asked the third time they crossed the same tunnel. They were a little further along each time, but it was late in her day and she was finally getting sleepy.

"Mostly because I have the nagging feeling that we're being followed." Constance held up a finger for silence and stopped walking.

They stopped, too—*and heard footsteps behind them!* Though the footsteps didn't stop, they slowed further and further until Constance motioned for them to start moving again.

"Is it the guards?" Imber swallowed hard and wished she'd brought her whip. She hadn't progressed to the flexible, razor-sharp suge yet. She also hadn't expected to need to defend herself in the inner regions.

"I don't know." Constance chewed on her lip briefly. "You two keep walking. Take the next right turn and the one after that. I'll…"

"No." Rolf's refusal seemed loud even though he'd whispered it. "I'll do it."

"Rolf, you haven't had any training," Constance began to object, but she was too late. It was a dim spot in the tunnel, one of the lightning globes having gone out, and he'd already flattened himself against a wall.

"We have to keep going." Imber moved a little away from Constance to make it seem like their group was still three fairies wide.

Reluctantly, Constance did just that, somehow resisting the urge to go back and shake some sense into the scrawny historian. She'd admired his courage on the *Falcon* when he refused to surrender his history book, but she also would never have hurt him. Their mysterious shadow might have different ideas.

"So help me," she smiled pleasantly, "if anything happens to him, I will personally chase the perpetrator into a mosquito-infested swamp."

Imber wanted to keep talking. To perpetuate the illusion that everything was normal. She just couldn't seem to get enough breath to speak. Constance's cold threat didn't help at all.

Abruptly, there came the sounds of a scuffle from behind them.

Chapter 14

"Rolf, let him up," Constance ordered briskly as soon as she got a look at the wrestling duo. Privately, she admitted that she was impressed with Rolf's skillful ambush. "I know who he is."

Rolf rolled off the fairy he'd caught and sprang to his feet.

"The desk clerk from the Camphor?" Imber frowned at him, puzzled.

"Why are you following us?" Constance demanded.

"To make sure no one else is." The clerk shot Imber an ugly look.

"Alright, you've done your job." Rolf stepped between him and Imber. "Now go tell whomever you report to that she's pledged to share in the galdu council's fate."

"Her?" The clerk sneered. "She's a Botere. They'd never punish her."

"Not even for treason?" Imber glared at him. "They've punished our peers for less."

"Hurry along." Constance ordered in her best captain's voice. She pointed back in the direction they'd come. "We're late and it's your fault."

His shoulders slumped, the clerk did as he was told.

Gathering her younger companions, Constance hustled them along the tunnel. They took their first right, then another, and stopped in front of a small shop.

Imber gripped Rolf's hand tightly as the door opened to let them in.

"Quickly."

Obeying the hoarse instruction, they slipped inside.

Cambrian appeared out of a shadow and embraced Constance warmly.

"I thought you were never going to get here."

"We'd still be out there, walking in circles," she pulled back, "if Rolf here hadn't captured the man tagging along after us."

"Tagging along?" Confused, Cambrian looked to Rolf for more information.

"It was just the desk clerk from the Camphor, but we didn't know that until I ambushed him." Rolf adjusted the strap on his historian bag to give himself something to do with his free hand. "It sounds more exciting than it was."

Cambrian blinked. Part of the reason he'd come along on this mission was to keep an eye on Rolf, whose aunt he had nearly married. Ambushing strange fairies in dim tunnels definitely hadn't been in the brochure.

"Poor Gari," chuckled a deep voice. Erdi emerged from behind a rack of knee-high boots.

"He should've left that to the others."

"Others?" Constance squinted at him suspiciously. "Do you mean that someone else was following us?"

"No, not following. Watching." Erdi drew a short line and a turn in the air between them, the route they'd originally planned to take. "From the Camphor to here, you were under constant observation."

Rolf's mind took the news a step further and he shifted uneasily from one foot to the other. Supposing someone had watched him fly away from the speaker's house with Imber? Well… The galdu were hardly going to enforce the Water Fairy law against flying. And the odds of Katilla being one of the watchers were slim. Very, very slim, he told himself.

Imber was having the same thoughts, though with less optimism. Thankfully, nothing of a particularly private nature had happened. Nevertheless, she had no doubt that Katilla would be jealous of her flying with Rolf. The same as Imber would be if their roles were reversed.

Belatedly, she realized they were all looking at her.

"So." Erdi scratched his chin. "This is how you will get us all to Triens, eh? By using a Botere?"

"We're not using her," Rolf interjected firmly. "She has agreed to take the council to

Cachora in her private train carriage."

Erdi stiffened. "The plan was to go to Triens."

"Yes, I know." Imber flipped her braid back over her shoulder and wished she'd had time to pin it up properly. "However, with only one carriage there isn't time to travel from one end of the seven regions to the other collecting your councilors."

"Those in the outer regions were coming in to Triens." He still wasn't convinced.

"On public transport that will still take too long." She shook her head. "Our only hope of getting all of you together in one place quickly enough to make a real difference is if we pick each councilor up and move on to the next in as straight a line as circumstances will permit."

"Have you already sent word to them to meet in Triens?" Rolf wanted to know.

"How?" Erdi shook his head. "The trains have all but stopped for the night."

"Which leaves the tracks clear for us. No, there isn't time for indecision." Imber ignored his scowl. "My carriage will be at the Cundi train yard in less than an hour. It won't be there long."

"I like her." Wynston chuckled from where he'd silently watched the whole exchange.

"And on this you will risk all of our lives?" Erdi's growl was a little less enthusiastic.

"I will face your fate with you." Imber

reiterated her pledge from earlier, this time without the heart bond.

Wynston nodded. "Let's go."

"Wait!" Cambrian read mild exasperation on Imber's face as he turned to Rolf. "You have to stay."

"What?" Rolf gripped Imber's hand even more tightly. "Why?" He flattered himself that he kept his tone reasonably level.

"The presentation of the history books, lad." Jennings got up from the dark corner where he'd been sprawled comfortably. "You and I," he looked at Imber a little sadly, "and Katilla have a presentation to make tomor…" He paused. Corrected himself. "Later today."

"I forgot about that." As much as it pained Rolf to admit it, that was the truth. He'd even forgotten that he still had to make updates to his history book. What was happening to him?

Imber clamped her lips shut against asking why Katilla would be helping with the presentation. She certainly couldn't argue that the other girl should come along to Cachora. The carriage would be overcrowded as it was.

"We'll keep working our way out to the Mugan region," Jennings reminded them. "Won't be soon, but we'll get to Cachora."

"This is good." Imber nodded a little too emphatically. "If everyone is focused on the upcoming presentations here and the high council meeting in Cachora, hopefully it will keep them from noticing a fast-moving carriage and a few missing galdu."

Wynston scratched his chin and concurred. "Makes sense."

"Aye, it all makes sense." Erdi heaved a heartfelt sigh. "Now if we just knew how to convince the others to go along with this…insane plan!"

"You yourself have agreed to this plan, Councilor Erdi," Cambrian answered mildly. "Surely that will give them confidence in it."

"I, a councilor?" Erdi blustered.

"It's a lot harder to fool someone who has also made a practice of concealing their authority." Cambrian cocked an eyebrow at him. "I'd say you're the councilor from the Muina region."

"He's the perfect candidate," Constance chimed in. "Who else can traverse all seven regions with no more trouble than having to humble himself enough to check in with city guards?"

Erdi grumbled some more, then finally yielded.

"Yes, I am a councilor."

"Very good. That saves us a trip to Muina." Imber smiled. "Shall we go?"

"Not all together." Erdi glanced around the group. "Pair up. A few twos walking about the tunnels won't catch the guards' eyes as easily as a bunch this size."

Constance and Cambrian left first. Then Wynston and Erdi.

Imber reached out and tugged on Rolf's jacket.

"You got all mussed fighting with that clerk," she sounded a little breathless as she dusted off his shoulders and straightened his collar. Suddenly, she went up on her toes and hugged Rolf lightly. "You should get back to the inn. Try to get some rest before the presentation."

Before he could even put his arms around her to return the hug, she was gone.

"I'll see that she gets to the yard safely," Jennings promised, and slipped out after her.

Alone in the dim room, Rolf raked his fingers through his hair. "What just happened?" He'd fully intended to walk with her himself.

He was working on the history book when Jennings returned to the inn.

"They're off safely." Jennings scrubbed a hand over his face. "You want anything before I go down?"

"Have you seen Katilla since I left for Imber's?" Rolf set aside his quill and flexed cramped fingers.

"She was supposed to go round up the councilor from Cundi." Jennings toed off his boots and set them by his bedroom door. "Don't know if she managed to or not."

"She did." Rolf's back popped as he got to his feet. "Count on it."

"Yeah, you're right." Jennings chuckled. "I asked the clerk to send up breakfast in a few hours."

"Great."

They waved wearily at each other and went into their respective rooms.

The next several days dragged by for Rolf, though he smiled politely, answered questions, and made presentations in Cundi and Pida. The closest they got to news of the galdu high council was a message from Lady Mari, offering the use of her carriage again.

Rolf politely declined this time, having learned that the public transport was a wonderful place to reshape the perspectives of the Water Fairies and galdu at large. He'd start by talking with Jennings or Katilla, then have the entire carriage involved in a conversation before the next stop.

As it turned out, only one in a thousand Water Fairies had ever visited the surface. And most of them had a bad impression of it.

"Bleak and barren," scoffed one who had taken a year of guard duty near a mountain portal.

"Full of fairy-eating monsters," asserted another.

Rolf drew each protest into the light and countered it with experiences from his own life.

If he couldn't, Jennings was only too happy to share a tale of his own, which gave Rolf a chance to relax.

As the train pulled into Lauga, capital city of the fifth region, Jennings observed quietly, "Seems like half the Water Fairies'd be just as happy on the surface as under the water."

"Or would at least appreciate having a choice in the matter." Rolf capped his water flask and stowed it as the doors opened. "Here we go again."

Katilla continued to refuse his help with her things, so Rolf juggled his own kit on the way to the baggage claim.

"Are you Historian Warner?" A tall, well-muscled Water Fairy guard stopped them.

"I am." Rolf didn't miss the three other guards fanning out around his group. "How can I help you?"

"You'll have to come with me to the bilera at once."

"What about our things?" Jennings started to protest, but Katilla tugged on his sleeve and shook her head.

"Only the historian will be coming with us."

Jennings looked at the other guards and snickered. "This is mighty obliging of you fellas. I haven't had a good scrap in weeks!"

"Jennings." Rolf's soft voice stopped the man where he stood, thankfully. Brawling with the city guards would do far more harm than good. "I'll meet you at the Cypress when I'm done, alright?"

"Come along." The guard closed up around Rolf and marched him away before Jennings could respond.

A galdu in the crowd was so busy muttering and shaking his head that he bumped into Katilla as he went on his way. She quietly moved aside, careful not to drop the piece of paper he'd pressed into her hand.

"Of all the…" Jennings was fighting mad. "They can't just take him away like that! Where's the writ? Where's the…"

"Not so loud." Katilla motioned to an employee from her father's inn. "Take our things to the Cypress," she instructed. Catching Jennings by the hand, she drug him over to the nearest wall and positioned him to shield her from casual observation while she read the note.

"They've detained the galdu council."

Jennings blanched. "On what charge?"

"I can think of a dozen without even trying." Katilla savagely crumpled the paper in her hand, then stuffed it in a secure pocket. "It could be worse."

"My prince and your…" Jennings stopped abruptly. "Why didn't they take you just now?"

"Like I said." Katilla peered around him. Nobody *seemed* to be paying them any special attention. "It could be worse."

"I'm hungry," she announced a moment

later. Taking his hand again, she headed for the market, not the Cypress.

"Um, me, too, but shouldn't we be—" He broke off abruptly when she zigged around a delivery cart.

"Trust me," she muttered as they paused at a tunnel crossing, waiting for a chance to merge into the heavy foot traffic.

Meanwhile, Rolf had just reached the bilera. His hopes dimmed as the guards marched him over to the left of the council table, the place reserved for troublemakers. The way the guard's hand rested heavily on his shoulder didn't help, either.

Some of the crowd they'd gathered on their way from the train yard were bold enough to take seats in the bilera's gallery, while others appeared to be simply curious passersby, drawn in by the feeling that something was about to happen.

He looked up in time to see the council members begin filing in and was surprised to see that some of their robes were askew. One of the women had her hair back in a mesh safety net, as though she'd left a scientific experiment hurriedly.

Interesting.

He put his hands behind his back and faced the six councilors squarely. The speaker's chair remained empty, for all the regional speakers were still at the high council in Cachora.

Once they were seated, the most senior councilor cleared her throat.

"Who stands before us?"

Rolf dropped his shoulder out from under the guard's hand and stepped forward. "Historian Rolf Warner."

The gallery's instant, whispered response told him he'd done something unusual.

"You dare address us directly?" The councilor stared down her nose at him and rapped on the table for the spectators to still themselves.

"My conscience is clear of offense." Rolf pretended the councilor was just one of the more crochety instructors at the historian academy he'd attended briefly. "Though that may be because the guard neglected to advise me of why I am here."

"You are here because we sent for you," snapped a junior councilor.

"Then which of us has committed the crime?" Rolf parried coolly. He'd learned a lot about Water Fairy law from Katilla. "Or is Ten'rae's illustrious regional council in the habit of interrupting the peaceful, private lives of guests from the surface?" Perhaps the most important thing he'd learned was that the bulk of their laws simply didn't recognize a fairy in his position, a cocheta. Not Water Fairy, not galdu, he was virtually untouchable. In theory.

"Your so-called private life, young man," the

senior councilor frowned at him, "has a very definite connection to the disruption of good order in the regions." She gestured and the guards faded away from around Rolf, taking up stations by the doors instead.

Rolf waited patiently in the silence rather than trying to fill it with words. She certainly hadn't asked him a question. And if she'd intended to accuse him, well, he undoubtedly had stirred things up.

It got so quiet that he fancied he could hear the sounds of the scribes' quills as they recorded the councilor's words.

A motion at the door to his left caught his eye and his mouth tightened. *Baron Razoi. What are you doing so far from home, I wonder?*

The councilor opened her mouth to speak again, then paused as another commotion swept through the gallery.

Six galdu fairies paraded into the chamber. Each of the women and men in the line stopped for a good look at the Water Fairy council, then walked to the front row of the gallery and took seats directly in its center. The galdu spectators already occupying those seats leapt out of their way, confirming their importance.

Suddenly nervous, Rolf had all he could to not to fidget. It was one thing to be on trial himself, especially on a trumped up bit of nothing like this. To have what could only be the galdu council for this city turn out in open defiance—there could be very, very serious consequences for their bravery.

How had they even known he…? The question was answered by the arrival of Jennings and Katilla, who promptly seated themselves by the galdu council.

"In what way," he turned sharply to the Water Fairy council, "have I contributed to the disruption of good order in your region? Has work been interrupted? Is the market closed? Or perhaps violent and disrespectful acts have been perpetrated against representatives of Water Fairy authority?"

Six councilors shifted uncomfortably in their seats.

"Of what, precisely, am I accused?" Rolf wanted to take another step forward, but resisted. The last thing he needed was for his impatience to be mistaken for aggression.

"You are guilty of inciting to insurrection." Unable to stand the council's delay any longer, Baron Razoi erupted from the corner where he'd planned to watch the fun.

"You are my accuser?" Of course he was. Rolf just wanted his statement on record.

"I am proud to say that I am," Razoi sneered.

"Proud?" Rolf cocked his head to one side and peered at the arrogant fellow. "Is this the way a Water Fairy feels when finding an injustice?"

The gallery responded before the council could and it took a prolonged table rapping to restore quiet.

"We will ask the questions, young man."

"By all means." Rolf offered a sweeping bow. "I look forward to them."

"You," the baron sputtered, "look forward to them?"

Rolf's answer was to give the man a puzzled look.

"We waste time here!" The baron approached the table, one arm raised and a finger pointed directly at Rolf. "This advena conspires to create discontent! He openly flouts his origin and tempts others with wild tales of the surface!"

"Which is it, Baron?" Rolf stroked his chin thoughtfully. "Do I make plans in deep shadows," he laughed because he most certainly had, "or do I publicly declare that the surface tribes are and have been at peace for generations?"

The baron's face turned a horrid shade of purple and just as he was about to answer, Rolf spoke again. "Or are you in fact upset because I speak an inconvenient truth?"

Chapter 15

"Truth?! Inconvenient?!" The baron raged incoherently, ignoring the insistent raps coming from the council's table.

Rolf bowed apologetically to the councilors. "I would like to ask for your permission," he spoke above the baron's raving, "to continue my conversation with the baron uninterrupted." The baron whirled to face him. "I am convinced," Rolf went on at a moderated volume, "that it will prove useful in determining whether I am innocent or guilty of inciting anyone to insurrection."

With difficulty, Rolf smiled while the councilors looked back and forth at each other.

"Very well."

"Thank you." Hardly resounding support of the idea, but he would take it. Rounding on the baron, who had unfortunately regained a semblance of self-control, Rolf baited him.

"Baron Razoi." Rolf folded his arms. "You see I am familiar with your correct title."

"As you should be." The baron smoothed his elaborate knot. Swaggered in place, his fashionably carved fishbone walking stick tucked briefly under one arm. "Water Fairy titles are bestowed on merit, not lineage."

"That is true." Rolf paced a few steps to his left. Gaze fixed somewhere in the distance, he asked, "What was your contribution to the sciences that won you the honor of your title?"

Razoi's chest puffed visibly, stirring the ruffles on his shirtfront. "I unlocked the secrets of Uraren Sukarra, a deadly, water-born disease."

Judging by the mutterings in the gallery, Rolf concluded that calling it 'deadly' was too polite. "Unlocked the secrets? Could you be more specific, sir?"

"I think you mean, can I use smaller words." The baron sneered at him. "Very well. For the simple-minded among us," he strutted toward the gallery, "it was I who found a way to defeat the virus that killed thousands each year."

"I applaud your skills, sir." Rolf bowed to him, ignoring his insults and wishing that the noisy gallery would do the same. "However, I fail to understand how someone as intelligent as yourself, someone who clearly values fairy life," he resumed his pacing, forcing the baron to turn bodily in order to keep looking at him, "can be satisfied with the present standard of life in the seven regions."

"This!" The baron pointed at him with both hands this time, nearly dropping his walking stick. "This is what I spoke of!" Holding his hands plaintively out at his sides, he nearly bellowed, "He maligns our way of life!"

"I've done no such thing." Rolf's quiet word was loud in the ensuing hush. "How could I possibly insult your fine cities? Your amazing educational system? Your dedication to honor and truth?" His tone changed subtly as he finished, turning the last accolade into an implied criticism of the baron personally.

Stepping around the man, Rolf addressed the gallery. "I would that every fairy in Fairydom had access to these things."

The spectators erupted in cheers, then hushed as he held up his hands.

"I also would see every fairy free to come and go among the tribal lands." Spinning, he moved in close to the baron. "Free to drink in the beauty and bounty of the land and the seas."

"You claim to hold our ways in esteem." The baron's voice shook with rage. "Then almost in the same breath you have the temerity to suggest we share our knowledge, *our* skills with these, these drudges?!"

Rolf's eyes narrowed. He'd expected the baron to directly attack the idea of dissolving the treaty. To prate about tribal security and claim the surface was still at war. Caught unprepared by his blatant prejudice, Rolf scrambled to mentally regroup.

"Ha!" The baron's voice echoed in the silent bilera. "They are not fit to enter our laboratories. Except to clean them!"

"Is that a fact?" A voice rang out from the crowd and an otherwise plain young man with flaming pink hair moved away from the wall of the bilera. Rolf suddenly realized that the chamber had filled to overflowing. "Is that how you see me, Baron Razoi? As a drudge?"

Rolf stared back and forth between them, completely confused. Then, the young man looked at him and Rolf gasped. For underneath the stranger's shock of pink hair were vivid *green* eyes! As he looked around those who'd arrived too late to claim a seat, Rolf saw over a dozen fairies with pink hair and different colored-eyes that declared their mixed tribal heritages beyond a shadow of a doubt.

"Gutxri." The name was a snarl on the baron's lips.

"Scholar Gutxri. Or do you deny the title the regional council of Seyth bestowed upon me, cousin?"

"It was a mistake." Razoi began shaking his head violently. "A grave error in judgement."

"A mistake? Granting me a title that I merited through my own hard work?" Gutxri moved closer. "Or elevating fairies like me from our roles as *drudges*?"

Razoi flinched visibly. "You are drudges. That's why you're here. You came to us, gifts from the sea." He clawed at his neckcloth as though he was having trouble breathing. "We were born to the sciences. It is our birthright!" As if to punctuate his point, he swung his walking stick in a wide, sweeping arc that nearly connected with Gutxri's chest.

"Freedom is the birthright of all fairies." Speaker Petua Actare, apparently recovered from her aching hip, stood tall in the entrance to the bilera. "I, too, would see all fairies freed to enjoy a united Fairydom. In the past, the terms of our treaty with the surface tribes forced us to make a terrible choice."

The gallery buzzed with questions while staying quiet enough to listen.

Likewise, Rolf's head buzzed with questions. Why wasn't Speaker Actare in Cachora? Was the high council over? What had they decided? Where was Imber? And the galdu high council, of course.

Speaker Actare lifted one hand. "We could watch survivors of windship crashes die of injury and starvation. We could wait and hope that curious miners and colonists never discovered our hidden portals." Unchallenged by the seated regional council, Speaker Actare moved further into the bilera and raised her other hand, mimicking a common set of scales in perfect balance. "Conversely, we could give in to paranoia and exterminate every single fairy on the surface at the slightest conceivable provocation." Her second hand fell to her side as if under the great weight of her words.

"So you chose the third option," Rolf inserted boldly. He saw their decision clearly for the first time. It was just like Cambrian tried to tell Erdi before. "You detained surface fairies as you deemed necessary." It made a sad, logical sort of sense.

"Yes." Speaker Actare nodded miserably.

"However." A man moved up beside her, his body bent with age, his brown hair faded to tan, keen eyes raking the gallery. "We were not born to serve as drudges."

"No." Another voice cut through the murmurings. An elegantly dressed man seated himself in the speaker's chair at the council table. At his gesture, two attendants quickly brought seats for Speaker Actare and the mysterious galdu with her.

"Which is why," the speaker resumed as soon as they were seated, "the Water Fairy and Galdu high councils have unanimously decided to work toward a time when our portals may be reopened, granting access to the seven regions and the surface to all fairies."

Rolf listened in growing surprise. Wasn't this the speaker who lodged a formal complaint and tried to avoid participating in the high council? This was quite a change of heart!

"No." Razoi shifted his grip on his walking stick, tilting the tapered, metal-tipped end up menacingly. "You have no right!"

"The high council has every right to make tribal decisions." Yet another fairy came forward to stand beside the council table, the chain of office about her neck marking her as a regional speaker as well.

Rolf shook his spinning head. Had the entire high—had *both* high councils somehow found out he was on trial and come to rescue him? The absurd thought nearly made him laugh aloud.

"No. No, you're all traitors! To our tribe! To the treaty!" Razoi pointed his walking stick at the ones he could see. "You care nothing about our ways! What will happen?" He advanced toward the council table until two guards moved to intercept him. "What will happen if they leave? Have you thought of that? Do you honestly expect Water Fairies to leave their pursuit of knowledge and excellence to…to wash dishes?!" His voice was hoarse with disbelief.

"These advena," he jerked around to indicate the gallery, almost decapitating his cousin in the process, "have never seen the surface. Not really. Some work the island farms and yes, they gather to tell each other fine tales of a world they don't actually know." Raking his hands through his hair, he asked, "What loss is it if they stay to serve us? Tell me!! Do you stand there ready and willing to *cripple* our tribe for the convenience of these…" Words failed him.

The older man sitting next to Speaker Actare motioned calmly to the angrily muttering gallery and it mercifully stilled.

"Baron Razoi." Ten'rae's speaker got to his

feet. "You have unjustly accused Historian Rolf Warner of," he checked the notes of the councilor to his right, "inciting to insurrection. Do you wish to pursue that accusation properly?"

The six other councilors at the table lowered their gazes in embarrassment. By Water Fairy law, they shouldn't have attempted to proceed with a trial while the regional speaker was away. The baron persuaded them that the situation was urgent, but none of them had the courage to insist on a formal investigation prior to agreeing to the trial.

"Do I...?" The baron laughed. "You think..." He laughed again, much harder.

The hairs on the back of Rolf's neck stood on end and he moved without thinking, a mere fingers' width ahead of the baron's sudden attack with his walking stick. Rolf ducked and dodged, rolling desperately aside while the crowd surged forward to watch, forming a solid wall of bodies that hemmed them in.

The sheer numbers of fairies in the way prevented the guards from reaching the baron.

When he caught the metal tip of the baron's stick in the base of his wings, Rolf knew it was time to change tactics. Ripping off his ever-present historian's bag, he threw it in the general direction of the council table for safe-keeping.

Challenging the baron bare-handed was out

of the question. His erratic swings and lunges were fueled by insanity. Instead, Rolf faced him. Took a hit to his ribs that felt like it cracked something and grabbed the stick with both hands.

Leaping into the air, Rolf let the baron's wild jerk on the stick knock the man off his own feet while pulling Rolf along as he stumbled backwards. Planting his feet again, Rolf lashed out, striking the baron sharply in his soft middle.

And went flying as the baron shook his walking stick violently. Rolf's hips and shoulders hit the floor of the bilera and he watched numbly as the stick came plunging down toward his chest.

Hands wrapped themselves around Rolf's wrists, hauling him out of the way. He saw a vaguely familiar face—Gutxri?—which he sensed belonged to the hands pulling him to safety and…

Someone screamed as the walking stick's metal tip penetrated Rolf's upper thigh.

It stayed there as the guards, who'd finally fought their way through the crowd, subdued a wildly resisting Razoi.

"Rolf!"

He heard a familiar voice calling to him but couldn't take his eyes off the white walking stick protruding from his leg.

"Out of the way there!" Jennings was close

to knocking heads together by the time he'd shoved aside enough gawking onlookers to reach the lad.

"Rolf." Imber was there, holding his hand. "Get an aid kit!" she snapped at a lurking guard. "And clear this crowd!"

"The crowd's bein' cleared," Jennings retorted from where he was inspecting the wound. "Let the councils handle that."

"Can I help?" Gutxri dropped to one knee beside Rolf.

"You already have." Rolf extended his hand to the man who'd pulled him away from a death blow. "Thank you for saving my life."

"It was little enough to do." Gutxri gripped his hand. "I should've fought him myself."

Rolf laughed. Yes, laughed!

"With what, Scholar Gutxri?" He knew full well that many Water Fairies studied fighting as a form of physical self-control, but had the feeling Gutxri wasn't among them.

"Here's the aid kit," announced the guard as he returned.

"Thank you. Now bring me a cart." Imber opened the kit and scanned its contents with a trained eye. "A smooth-riding cart if it's to be had and long enough for a fairy to lie down on."

"I… Yes." Though the guard didn't look too hopeful, he left anyway.

"Hello." Rolf wondered vaguely where—and when—Gutxri had gone, but most of his concentration was on Imber. She helped take his mind off the pain. "What are you doing here?"

"Hello yourself." Imber inserted a needle into his thigh muscle, injecting something to relieve his pain and protect against infection. "Jennings, I need your neckcloth."

"Never thought I'd live to see the day one of these was actually useful." Jennings muttered as he removed the offending item.

"Wrap it around his leg above the cane. Not too tightly." To Rolf she whispered, "This is going to hurt." There was nothing else she could do, of course. The cane had to come out and without a tourniquet, he could bleed to death.

"Ready." Jennings, no stranger to injuries, had applied the makeshift tourniquet deftly.

Imber moved so that she was between Rolf and Jennings. Gripped Rolf's shoulders and shifted so that her weight was where it would do the most good.

"Now." She held Rolf steady when Jennings pulled the cane out. Blotted the sweat from Rolf's forehead with her sleeve. "That was the worst part," she promised. She certainly hoped so. She usually wasn't the squeamish type, but her stomach was lodging fearsome complaints.

"Here's the cart." Jennings gently lifted Imber and set her to one side. "Bear a hand, fellas." The few remaining spectators were quick to form up around Rolf, hefting him onto the cart.

Imber collected the aid kit before it could get stepped on, then stood on the lower shelf of the cart.

Jennings walked along behind her to keep her from falling off while she cleaned the wound.

"Talk to me."

"About what?" Good grief, she was struggling to open the pouch of liquid wound cleanser and Rolf expected her to make conversation?

The cart hit a rough spot and his face went even paler, if that was possible.

"Umm..." Feverishly, she tried to think of something to say. *Anything* to take his mind of what was happening. *I'm falling in love with you?* No, not that. "What am I doing here? Well, that's an interesting story." At least, she hoped so.

"We made it as far as Cachora, all seven galdu councilors and myself." Plus one little girl who refused to let Mommy leave without her. She spread a clean cloth over the wound and soaked it with the solution, "we all agreed that the galdu would like to return to the surface. No surprise there."

"I sense a surprise coming, though," Rolf coaxed, gripping both sides of the cart and trying not to worry about the fact that he no longer had any feeling in his injured leg.

"What gave it away?" she teased. The color was coming back into his face, so she hoped the wound site was finally numb. "Erdi made us comfortable at one of his inns—I believe the man has one in all seven capital cities—and we tried to think what we should do next. The Water Fairy high council was meeting behind closed doors, you see, out of our reach."

To keep her hands busy now that she'd done what she could with the wound, she tentatively smoothed his hair. "The third day, my grandmother came to the inn and personally invited us to meet with the Water Fairy high council."

"And you said that couldn't happen." He risked letting go of the table to touch her face.

"Yeah, I guess I did." She rested her cheek against his palm. "Everyone got along pretty well after the first round of arguments." Somehow it didn't seem like the right time to tell Rolf how close they'd all come to standing trial for their illegal activities. "You need a haircut," she observed irrelevantly. As she wound a finger in a lock of his hair she hoped he was as distracted as she was.

"I think you're right," he agreed with a faint smile.

"Off you get." Jennings plucked Imber from the cart as if she were weightless. "Time to let the doctors have a peek at ya, lad."

"I'd like to assist you, Doctor." Imber announced boldly to the woman examining Rolf's wound.

"Credentials?" The doctor patted Rolf's hand reassuringly. "Nurse, prepare a length of starfish tubing."

"I'm studying under my grandmother, Lady Mari Botere," Imber answered at once.

The doctor's head came up sharply. "Good. The nurse will help you get ready."

Jennings cleared his throat after Imber left. "Will he be alright, Doc?" What he wouldn't have given for a familiar face right then!

The woman blinked and for the first time really looked at the mixed group of fairies who'd brought her patient in. Smiled reassuringly.

"What struck him?" The narrow hole in his leg went right through the muscle and pierced his artery. She would have to widen the hole in order to repair the artery, but the starfish tubing would do the job once she got in there.

"This." Jennings held up the walking stick. He'd almost thrown it several times on their way to the hospital, but something made him hang onto it each time.

"That?" The doctor frowned as she examined it. The odd choice of weapon made her think the attack must have been spontaneous. She accepted a pair of scissors from a nurse and started cutting Rolf's pant leg off. "It missed the bone. Once we repair the artery, he'll be fine in a couple of days." She paused to give Rolf's arm a final pat. "Providing you don't neglect your medications."

"Jennings." Rolf caught his friend by the arm as the nurses tried to wheel him away. "My history book. I—it's still in the bilera, I think. Will you find it and take care of it for me, please?"

"Oh, you think you can just send me after it, eh? Am I an errand boy now?" Jennings scoffed, mussing the hair that Imber had so tenderly put in place. "Well, why not? I'm already chief cook and bottle washer. So go on, go on! Go lie flat on yer back while I do all the work around here."

"Thanks, Elihu." Despite everything, Rolf chuckled when Jennings grimaced at the use of his first name.

Chapter 16

"Here, hold this." Rolf handed his cane to Jennings in exchange for the final history book.

"You shouldn't do that," Imber warned, coming up beside him on the grandstand. It was nearly two weeks since his injury in Ten'rae, and he was making progress, but a wound this deep took extra time and care to heal. At least, that was the excuse she kept giving for traveling with him all the way to Cachora.

"I know, Doctor, I know." He grinned, loving the way her cheeks went as pink as her hair when he used her new title. She was already working on mastering a second subject, something to do with plants.

"Stubborn," she muttered just loudly enough for him to hear as he turned to face the assembly. He looked much better now that he'd finally agreed to let her cut his hair. She'd lost track of how many times she'd had to offer, though.

"My friends!" Rolf stopped in the center of the stage. His leg would hold; for now. "This is the last history book to be presented in the seven regions." He held the history book aloft while they cheered, then handed the book to the young man standing beside him.

"Thank you." Clutching his prize, the boy hurried down the stairs to where his family was anxiously waiting.

"But that is not the last of the history we will make today." Rolf held his hand out to Imber. Instead of putting her hand in his, she pressed his cane into it and he accepted it with a suppressed grimace. "It is my privilege to introduce to you Doctor Imber Botere, who has an official announcement to make on behalf of the Water Fairy high council."

"Ladies and gentlefairies." Imber hid her nerves behind a full smile. They could have chosen anyone in Cachora to make this announcement. The council speaker, for example. But no, someone had to suggest that this announcement would come best from one of the younger Water Fairies, as pointing to a harmonious future.

An impetuous one, too, in her opinion. The councils never moved this swiftly!

"It is my great pleasure," she kept smiling, "to inform you that arrangements are being made to open our portals this spring."

The force from the cheers blew her back a step. Rolf's free hand settled on her elbow, steadying her. She happily retreated to stand with him, clearing the way for the speaker, who did have several more announcements to make.

The best part about the moment, though, was that everyone was applauding. It wasn't just one tribe. It wasn't even just the galdu. Imber had to blink away the tears that threatened. Botere didn't cry; not in public, at any rate.

Cachora's speaker raised his hands for their attention and waited patiently for the jubilation to quiet down.

"We have waited a long time for this, my friends." The elderly man paused for the last few to settle enough to listen. "To help us prepare for the reuniting of the tribes, many things will change. I will now explain a few of these things, with more information to come as our councils work together," he motioned for his galdu counterpart to join him, "to bring these changes about. Beginning tomorrow in every city of the Mugan region, times will be designated for those who wish to practice flying. Also, meetings will be held to discuss the opportunities available on the surface, including new occupations and skills."

The galdu speaker picked up the thought by saying, "Allow me to present Captain David Watts, lately of the surface. He and his men will be…"

The rest of the speaker's words were lost in the pursuant uproar as David and two of his crew members flew out from behind the partition where they were waiting and hovered briefly before settling on the stage. He'd assigned an officer to each region and still worried that there was too much to get done in the mere weeks before spring arrived.

Rolf felt Imber's hand slip into his own and squeezed it gently. Given the choice, he would've tried to coax her into leaving the meeting with him. They needed to talk. Unfortunately, as the resident Silver Fairy Historian, he was obligated to remain. In fact…

"Here you go." Jennings set a table in front of him.

Someone else placed a chair behind him.

"Thank you." Reluctantly releasing Imber's hand, Rolf seated himself and selected a quill from the bag Jennings held out.

He left recording Captain Watt's speech word-for-word to the scribes, whom he'd discovered were incredibly good at their jobs. And he'd have to wait to collect precise numbers from the guards who were in position to direct traffic, that sort of thing.

On this, the one hundredth day of the reign of King Hugh and Queen Rebecca of the Silver Fairy Tribe, an assembly was held in Cachora, the capitol city of Mugan, the seventh region of the Water Fairies.

He worked on, busily capturing living history until someone called his name.

"Rolf? Can you hear me?"

Looking up, he smiled sheepishly. He'd done exactly what he was trained to—remained aware of what was happening without being part of it. That was a very necessary skill for an historian; but sometimes it had awkward results.

"Katilla!" Coming to his feet, he gave her a quick hug. "How are you?"

Pockets of trouble had cropped up all over the seven regions when it became public knowledge that a Water Fairy Baron was being held for attacking a cocheta. A few other Water Fairies were also arrested for defying the high council, and Katilla, along with many others, had spent the last twelve days spreading the truth of the happenings, calming things down.

"I'm well, thank you." She bit her lip. "It's been so long…" Her voice trailed off. "Are you well?"

"Oh, I'm fine. Yes, life's rather dull right now. Just a lot of sitting on trains and standing on stages," he laughed.

"Yes, I've heard." She raised her eyebrows to let him know she was not amused at being teased. "And your leg?"

"Making wonderful progress." He held out his empty hands. "See? I hardly need the cane anymore."

"Oh sure." Jennings seized the moment to start packing things up, knowing that if he hesitated, Rolf would sit down and be lost in his work again. "Like in Renna?"

"I heard about that." Katilla retrieved his cane and held it out to him. "You nearly fell off the stage."

"That's an exaggeration." He protested even as he gingerly accepted the cane from her.

He had the funny feeling that she wanted to smack him with it.

"Not much," muttered Jennings as he folded up the table. "Can we go now?"

"Don't mind him." Rolf winked at Katilla. "He always gets in a mood when he's hungry."

"Will you listen to him?" Jennings passed the chair off to the lad he'd hired to carry their things. "That's it, thank ya." Returning his attention to Katilla, he looped a brotherly arm around her shoulders. "If I had a llow for every time he's wished for a good meal, I could find myself a nice little island and finally have a bit of peace."

"You'd be bored in a week," asserted Rolf with a laugh. Movement on his left caught his eye and he turned to find a rather pale Imber standing almost as though she'd frozen mid-step. "Imber. We're going to the Parota for lunch. Won't you join us?"

Imber looked from him to Katilla. The Parota was one of Erdi's inns, for one thing. For another, well—Katilla might prefer to have Rolf to herself. Imber had just spent twelve days with him aboard her carriage. As her patient, of course.

Katilla's mouth tightened. "You'd be most welcome at the table, Doctor."

"That's very kind of you." Imber finished taking her step and summoned up a smile. Which apparently didn't fool Rolf, if the slight narrowing of his eyes was any indicator.

"However, I'm afraid I can't. My grandmother is arriving shortly and I must be at the train yard to greet her."

"Another time, perhaps." Katilla noticed the faint frown on Rolf's face and allowed Jennings to 'distract' her with his hoped-for menu.

"You didn't tell me that your grandmother was coming." Rolf moved closer to Imber.

"I only received the signal this morning."

"And if I'd been there for breakfast like I have been, you would've had time to tell me all about it." Rolf sighed. "Imber, I can't stay in the carriage with you now that I'm nearly well again."

"I should say not," she agreed swiftly.

"Then…" His brow furrowed. "What's wrong?"

Wearily, she brushed a hand over her eyes. "They're waiting for you."

"They're my friends, they won't mind waiting a minute."

"Not now, Rolf." She looked away from his searching eyes. "Please."

He opened his mouth to ask when, but Jennings cleared his throat.

"Doctor Botere?" A Water Fairy lass ran lightly up the stairs. "Message from the train yard."

"Thank you." Imber took the slip of folded paper and pressed a llow into the girl's palm. "I have to go," she told Rolf. Without another word, she spread her wings and glided off the grandstand.

"Ain't she something?" The young girl tentatively flexed her own wing muscles.

"It's hard to be patient, isn't it?" And Rolf didn't just mean about learning to fly. How long would it take before Imber was ready to talk to him? "Better wait a while, though. You wouldn't want to damage your wings, would you?"

"No, sir." The lass shook her head vigorously.

"Are you comin'?" Jennings was getting impatient.

"That's a silly question." Rolf winked at the girl. "Want a lift?"

Her eyes went as big as saucers and she nodded emphatically.

"Off we go!" He put his arm around her waist, extended his wings, and coasted down to the mouth of the nearest tunnel. "What do you think?" He released her as soon as they were both steady on their feet again. "Do you like flying?"

"I love it!" she burst out.

"Wonderful. Keep up your exercises and you'll be at the top of your class when the time comes," he promised.

"Thank you, Historian!"

Rolf's chuckle died in his throat when he

looked up—and into Imber's eyes. She dropped her gaze instantly. Gathered her skirts and disappeared into the tunnel that led to the train yard.

"Pity we can't fly all the way to Parota." Jennings' big hand clamped down on Rolf's shoulder in time to keep him from pursuing Imber and demanding she tell him what was wrong.

"I'm just glad they're allowing flying at all." Katilla wrapped her wings around herself, then folded them back into place. "It's already hard to believe we ever lived without it."

Linking an arm with each of the men, she started them down the tunnel to the Parota.

"So, tell us what we've missed." Rolf dove into the conversational pool. "Were you able to settle things down?"

Katilla considered the question. "I didn't know if we would be able to at first. But being there to tell them what was happening made a lot of difference." She blew out a breath. "We went in groups, as you know. Galdu, Water Fairy, and where possible, we worked with someone from the city who was a descendant of both tribes."

"Right smart of you." Jennings nodded his approval. "Seems like that'd set folks minds at ease."

"It helped a lot," she agreed.

She filled the rest of their walk with stories

of her experiences, most of which involved someone named Miles.

"You must've been in Urbs for several days," Rolf suggested as she finished her fourth such story.

"No, just one. We had to go straight from there to Gero. Some of the richer Water Fairies were telling everyone that the high council reversed its decision and…" She gave a whole body shiver. "We almost had to call in regional guards."

Rolf's throat tightened painfully. If they'd done that, the guards wouldn't have been able to contain the resulting uproar. And, once order *was* painfully restored, no amount of talking could've repaired the damage to the galdu's fragile trust.

Jennings whistled softly as he opened the Parota's front door. "What a mess."

"That's not even the whole story. Why, without Miles' help, I think we'd still be there arguing."

"Oh, so he went with you to Gero." Rolf waved at Erdi, who was waiting in the lobby.

"Took you long enough." The big man grinned at them all. "Come on in! We've got two dozen fairies ready to hear all the news."

Rolf was more than happy to let Katilla and Jennings carry the conversational torch throughout the meal. He'd done enough public speaking over the last month to last a lifetime!

And though this was cunningly designed as a free meal, there were far too many questions for it to qualify as relaxing time with friends.

Besides, he was busy watching Miles watch Katilla. The fact that the handsome young man chose to follow her from the fourth region clear to the seventh told Rolf quite a bit about his feelings for her.

When the last of the dishes had been cleared away and the party broke into groups to discuss everything they'd heard that evening, Rolf made a point of selecting a seat a little off to one side. He didn't have a lot of experience with girls or the men that were interested in them, but he preferred privacy for serious discussions.

Sure enough, Miles wandered over in his direction.

"It came as quite a shock." Miles stared at Rolf. "The news that a baron attacked you."

"It's the other leg." Rolf pointed to his left leg. "I wish I could say I was shocked."

"What do you mean?" Miles' eyebrows went up and the corners of his mouth turned down.

"Um, just that…" Rolf shoved his fingers through his hair. What *did* he mean? "Maybe it's because I'm not from the seven regions, I don't know. But I didn't stop to be surprised that I was being attacked by a baron. If that makes sense?"

Miles took a sip of his nectar and mulled the statement over. "Yes, I think it does." He laughed bitterly. "I suppose I shan't be surprised by anything after this. The behavior of our smartest, most celebrated fairies hasn't been at all in keeping with the Water Fairy culture I was raised to be a part of."

"If I've learned anything in studying history it's never to judge an entire culture by the few who make the history books." Rolf gripped the arms of his chair tightly. "We only recently discovered that the fairy behind all the pirate activity on the surface was the king's champion."

"King's champion?" Miles shook his head. "I don't know what you mean."

"The king's champion is someone who is willing to stand in his place if a combat challenge is ever made," Rolf explained. "Highly skilled with many weapons and, usually, loyal to a fault. Bullierd was an exception to that last, I'm afraid."

"Miles?" Katilla's curiosity had gotten the better of her. "Rolf? You both look far too serious for a celebration."

"Yes, you're right!" Miles lifted his glass as if to offer a toast, then paused to check it. "Empty, worse luck. I'll just go get it refilled." He bowed to them both and headed for the table.

"Nice fellow." Rolf swirled his own remaining sip of nectar. "I quite see why you like him."

Katilla blushed. "I didn't say I like Miles."

"It's in your tone every time you speak his name." Rolf drained his glass and got to his feet.

"You're not leaving?" Katilla asked when he reached for his cane.

"I must." Rolf shrugged a trifle apologetically. "All this sitting is making my leg ache."

"I can have the fiddler call a tune," she suggested facetiously.

Chuckling, Rolf gave her a quick shoulder hug. "Next time, I hope."

"Rolf?"

He turned back to her, surprised by the uncertainty in her voice.

"You're going to see Imber, aren't you."

"The train yard is a decent walk from here." He didn't commit himself either way because he wasn't sure yet.

"She's a nice girl." Katilla touched his arm lightly. "I mean that."

"If I see her, I'll tell her you said so." Taking her hand, he kissed it softly. Then, as discreetly as he could manage with his cane, he left via the rear kitchen door.

He flew as often as he could on his way to the train yard, though he forced himself to walk as well.

"Never thought I'd long for a potion," he

chuckled as he paused to stretch his healing muscles. Water Fairy medicine had saved his leg, but even the simplest healing potion on the surface would've served to speed up his overall healing.

Predictably, the two carriages were parked end to end on an out-of-the-way siding. He debated briefly, then knocked on the door to Mari's carriage.

Mari opened the door, a sad expression on her face. "Come in, Rolf."

"Thank you." Smiling, he entered. And found Imber scowling at a series of signal slips laid out before her on one of the tables. "If this is a bad time, I can come back later."

"Sit, Rolf, sit." Mari indicated an empty chair and lowered herself into another one. "We've just gotten some bad news."

"Atrocious." Imber rubbed her forehead as if it hurt. "Atrocious news." There were certain disadvantages to having a lightning wire station in one's personal train carriage. Like always being accessible.

"From the surface?" he guessed.

"Yes." Mari closed her eyes. "You know we sent a doctor to Weetu to assess Prince Isaac's injuries."

"I do. A very generous gesture."

Mari smiled faintly. "After the high councils met, it was agreed that a small delegation should also be sent to the Wood Fairies in preparation for spring."

"Preparation for spring?" Rolf leaned forward in his chair. "I don't understand. How could anyone have gotten from the seven regions to Weetu in the middle of winter?"

"They swam." Imber shrugged slightly at his incredulous expression. This wasn't the time to go into how dangerous their journey had been.

"To the middle of the Great Woods?" Rolf wished he had a map so he could figure out exactly how far that was from…

"We have underwater portals, also. For our swimmers," Imber explained. "They were able to travel to an outpost by rail, then transfer to the water for the rest of their journey."

"You never cease to amaze me." He hastily turned to look at Mari as he spoke, to make it appear that he was referencing the entire tribe. Not just Imber. His smile faded as he met Mari's sad eyes. "Why am I just hearing about this now? What has gone wrong?"

Chapter 17

"Don't tell me they have rejected your diplomatic overtures." Rolf shook his head vehemently. "I know King Walter and Queen Fiona too well to believe that."

Mari exchanged a look with Imber, then sighed.

"You are right." Mari's mouth worked, but no more words came out. She simply couldn't bring herself to speak the words a second time that evening.

"We sent three representatives. Councilor Volt Clark, my uncle. Tri-Baron Duncan Edgins, of Seyth. And," Imber's tongue stuck to the roof of her mouth and she had to force it to move so that she nearly spat the last name, "Sir Derrick of Ten'rae." As she continued, her voice was barely above a whisper. "Unbeknownst to us, Sir Derrick took a vial containing a deadly virus with him."

Rolf's mouth went dry.

"Several days ago, he attempted to infect the entire city of Weetu." Mari picked up the story, her own voice hoarse with emotion. "A sympathizer of Baron Razoi's, Derrick also held the treaty paramount and believed the galdu were not his equals."

Imber finally reached out and touched Rolf's hand. Finding it icy cold, she wrapped her fingers around it.

"His treachery was discovered in time. Weetu is safe," she promised.

"Everyone in Weetu?"

His eyes burned into Imber's and she couldn't think to answer.

"There was one fatality." Mari examined the signal slips, looking for one in particular. "We immediately sent instructions for Sir Derrick to be held for trial and punishment. This was their answer." Finding the right slip, she turned it around so Rolf could read it.

Sir Derrick has already been punished. He is dead.

Rolf clung to Imber's hand as he worked to process the information. His knowledge of Wood Fairy law was spotty at best. He could recall nothing on the subject of the death penalty. For this attack, however, King Walter might have made a special decree.

And yet, if King Walter had been rash enough to order Sir Derrick's immediate execution, what would the Water Fairies do? They still had the power to decimate the surface population.

"My cousin was injured in the duel." Imber used her free hand to push another slip toward him. "But she's receiving excellent care and will recover."

"Your cousin?" Rolf scrambled to remember the doctor's name. "Lady Cassidy?

She *dueled* Sir Derrick? And won?" Then King Walter hadn't…

"That's right." Imber's gaze dropped, returned to his, then lowered again. "I'm anxious to visit her in Weetu." If she wasn't still upset with Rolf, she would've smiled at the thought that they might somehow meet at Weetu. He could show her the city and—but no. Her hurt pride still stung whenever Jennings' words came to mind.

"She'll be well long before spring," he assured her, squeezing her hand.

"Because of their medicinal potions?" Imber tried wriggling her fingers to no effect.

"Exactly." He grinned confidently. "I've had occasion to use every variety of potion," much to his cautious mother's dismay, "and I guarantee they are effective."

"I'm glad to hear that." Imber tugged at her hand and put it in her lap when he released it.

"Prince Isaac sends his regards." Mari discreetly sorted through the slips as though she hadn't noticed the disappointment on Rolf's face just now. "Rolf, I believe he expects you and Prince Cambrian to visit Weetu as well."

Rolf's eyes darted to Imber's face, but there was no telltale blush this time. Hadn't she known that when she hinted she was going to Weetu? Then why…? And…?

Deflated, he sat back. Oh bother. One day, when his little sisters were older, he needed to ask Jennifer and Juliette to explain women to him. Belatedly he realized that he hadn't answered Mari.

"I'll have to check with my aunt." He'd assumed he would resume his historian training, but now he wasn't sure. "Queen Rebecca."

"Of course." Mari stopped uselessly rearranging the signal slips. "How's your leg doing, Rolf?"

"Much better, thank you." He showed her the cane he was somehow still holding onto. "Imber says I'll be running again in no time."

"When did I say that?" She rose to his bait despite herself. Despite what she'd heard Jennings tell Katilla earlier.

"I distinctly recall you saying," he started to duck the question.

"When?" she repeated, not falling for his old trick.

"Well, I…"

"Alright, you two." Mari laughed and got to her feet. It was nearing the anniversary of her husband's passing and their banter made her miss him even more. "I've had a long day, so as much as I'd love to stay up and chat with you," she sent Imber a meaningful look, "I should probably get some sleep." She could tell something was troubling the girl and if it didn't involve the handsome historian, Mari would eat jellied squid.

"I'll bring you breakfast in the morning."

Imber rose and hugged her grandmother fiercely.

"Thank you dear, I'd love that." Mari sighed softly. "Unfortunately, I have to leave quite early tomorrow. The council has tasked me with the southern outpost." They'd also granted her authority to negotiate with the Plant Fairy Tribe, up to a point.

"That's such a long trip!" Imber pouted, then brightened as an idea struck her. "Would you like me to come with you?"

Rolf's stomach flipped at the thought of her leaving. Especially with the odd way she was behaving. They'd had such fun while traveling together. Hadn't they?

"We could couple our carriages and…"

"It's very sweet of you to offer," Mari interrupted, "but I'll be fine. In fact, I'll need the time to review the signal slips that keep pouring in." She gave Imber another hug. "You stay here and work on your flying. You might even talk with David and the windfairies to see what options are available on the surface. You'll get bored quickly if you're just visiting your cousin."

"You know me so well." Imber laughed and allowed herself to be politely escorted to the door.

"Thank you for your time, Lady Mari." Rolf bowed over her hand.

"Rolf." Mari flicked a glance over his shoulder to where Imber was hurrying toward her carriage. "We need all the help we can get right now. I know you're eager to return to your home, or at least, to the surface, but if you would consider staying on a few weeks past spring, we would appreciate it. Just long enough for us to welcome tribal ambassadors."

Rolf *did* want to go home. He missed the sky. The stars. The breezes. He even missed his little sisters. Especially the baby, Antoinette.

Strangest of all, he missed Imber. And she was only a stone's throw away.

"I serve at the pleasure of my queen," he said at last. "If I am not summoned elsewhere, I will gladly assist however I can."

"Thank you, Rolf." Mari patted his shoulder. "Now, you better go have a chat with my granddaughter."

Startled, Rolf took a half step back and nearly fell off the carriage steps. There was a rush of wind and Imber was suddenly by his side.

"Rolf! What happened? Was it your leg?"

He tried to answer, but she didn't stop talking long enough.

"You overdid it today, didn't you? Here, lean on me. We'll go to my carriage and I'll take a look at it. I think I still have everything I need." She'd sent most of the kit—and explicit instructions—with him when they arrived in Cachora.

Rolf went along meekly enough, though he

put his arm around her waist, not her shoulders. He watched the color come up in her cheeks as her conversation died down.

They made it all the way into her carriage before she moved away from him.

"Your leg's fine, isn't it?" she asked, hugging herself. Her heart was pounding and not from the exercise.

"It's been a little achy today." He hesitated, eyeing her closed posture. "Maybe you *should* take a look at it."

"Fine." Opening a cupboard, she produced a box of gauze wrap, ointments, and disinfectant. "Sit down."

"Hmm?" He leaned toward her, his mind still on what he wanted to say. And ask. "Oh! Oh. Yes." He sat and hastily reached to unbutton the flap of fabric they'd created in his least-favorite trousers. The wound was in an awkward spot, to say the least, and being able to simply move the flap made tending it much less troublesome.

"Wouldn't surprise me to see this turn up as the latest style," he joked, tapping the two large buttons that secured the flap. His fingertips barely brushed them when he was standing and he assumed they were mistaken for decoration by anybody who didn't know their true purpose.

"It might." She didn't feel like debating the point. Setting her things on the table she'd left in position, she sat beside him.

"I have worn it in, um…" He tried to remember how many cities he'd worn it in, but only came up with three out of the seven capitols and decided to let the subject drop. He had more important things on his mind, like not flinching when she probed the site.

"It's healing nicely," she announced, satisfied. "You might use a touch more salve tomorrow, though." Briskly, she repositioned the bandage and pinned it in place. "There."

Overcome with a sudden conviction that if she stood up, she'd walk away, he asked the first question that popped into his head.

"What do you want to do first when you visit the surface?"

Startled, she squinted at him. "Does it matter?" Collecting her supplies, she returned them to the cupboard. "I suppose the first thing you'll do is have a big meal." *Blast.* She hadn't meant to say that.

"I doubt it." First there would be all the formalities. A diplomatic delegation from each of the four surface tribes. An exchange of gifts. Speeches? Did he even have to ask? Of course there would be speeches.

He gave a wry smile, but she was still facing the cupboard, her shoulders rigid. Come to think of it, her wings were pressed tightly against her back as though…as though she were frightened. Or angry.

That didn't make sense. Did it? She couldn't

be afraid of him. Which meant she was angry. Maybe.

Standing up, he left his cane and made his way over to her. One thing he knew from his little sisters was that it was easier to understand them when he could look them in the eyes.

"Imber." He waited. "We can't fix it if we don't talk."

She brought one hand up to pinch the bridge of her nose. "What makes you think there's anything to fix?"

Instead of answering, he stole one of her hair pins. And another. Irritating his sisters was one absolutely guaranteed way to get them to talk to him, even if it started off as an argument.

"Rolf!" Spinning around, she put one hand up to her hair as it sagged under its own weight. "Don't do that!"

"I like it down better." He boldly freed another pin, adding it to the collection he was already holding out of her reach. "I especially liked the way you wore it this morning."

"Did you?" She scoffed and tried to walk away from him.

"Not so fast." He blocked her exit. Held out her pins as a peace offering. "I thought your hair was lovely this morning."

"Did you?" Her tone was completely different this time; softer, and a little hopeful. Yet doubt lingered in her eyes.

"You had one curl in particular that caught my eye." He took a strand of her loose hair in his fingers, accidentally dislodging even more pins that landed soundlessly on the carpeted floor. Her hair was as soft as corn silk. "It couldn't decide whether it wanted to nestle in with the others or tickle your cheek."

"Yes, I often have trouble making my hair mind." Somehow she managed to laugh as she stepped away from him.

"I've noticed." He had deliberately encouraged a certain level of formality between them while they were traveling alone, for both of their sakes. Tonight, however, he admitted to himself that she made a lovely picture, standing there using one of the windows as a mirror while she attempted to repair her hairdo.

Something in his tone made her heart shiver deliciously. They'd been alone every day since his injury and he'd never had this effect on her before. But then—she didn't think he'd ever tried before.

"You didn't tell me what you were going to do when you reach the surface." He stooped to gather the scattered hairpins despite a curious urge to close the gap between them.

"I…" She paused, one pin only halfway into her hair. "I don't know."

"You never told me what was wrong this morning, either." Crossing the carriage to her, he relinquished the rest of the hairpins.

"You'll think I'm silly."

"I could use a little silly." He smiled encouragingly. She probably could, too, after that news about Weetu and, um, whatever-his-name was.

"I heard Jennings," she accepted the pins from him slowly, "say that you were looking forward to a good meal."

"You're upset because I was hungry?" Perplexed, Rolf closed his hand over hers, mindful of the miniature daggers she was clutching.

"No." She tried to free her hand but this time he held firm. Exasperated, she blurted, "You didn't have to eat my cooking if you didn't want to!"

"What?" He released her. "Why wouldn't I eat your cooking? You make delicious food."

"I'm sure that's what you told," she caught back Katilla's name just in time, "Jennings."

"I did," he insisted. Thinking of a much better argument, he smugly folded his arms across his chest. "More importantly, have I ever failed to take seconds?"

She held up a finger, ready to dispute his remark, then stopped. Frowned.

"I've always taken seconds, haven't I?" He crowded her space, forcing her to tilt her head back to look up at him.

"Rolf." She bumped into the wall behind her and reflexively raised her hands to ward him off, the hair pins tumbling to the floor again. "I misunderstood."

"Here's something you definitely need to understand." He stopped a respectable distance away from her. "I care for you, Imber Botere."

Speechless, she stared up at him. This was *so* unexpected. She'd spent all day since the assembly looking for somewhere else to be, something else to do so she wouldn't have to watch Rolf with Katilla.

"I've wanted to tell you for a while." When she still didn't speak, he prompted, "Imber?"

"Rolf, we—" She shook her head, which already felt like it was spinning. "What do you want me to say? We're both so young." Too young, to be honest. Matching was decades away for her. If not a century!

"Yes, we are young." He agreed easily. "I'm over a decade away from offering a serious pledge, but…"

"Offering a pledge?" She jumped at the unfamiliar word, cocking her head to the side as she spoke, fully aware that she was interrupting. "What is that?"

Caught with his mouth open, he stared at her. "A pledge is…" He paused, thoroughly flummoxed. "Funny, I never really thought about it. That is, how to explain it."

"It sounds important." Having gained some time to think, Imber also managed a deep breath. "Perhaps we should ask Jennings to help explain it.”

Rolf winced. “I’d rather not.

“No?” She arched an eyebrow. “Doesn’t he know?”

“He knows.” Rolf blew out a breath. “There’s no doubt in my mind that he knows.” He also was absolutely certain that Jennings would find a way to tease him about it. They were friends, but Jennings was, well, himself. “You see, when two fairies …”

An errant giggle escaped her and he frowned.

“You know exactly what a pledge is, don’t you?”

She lifted both shoulders innocently. She hadn’t intended to giggle. Couldn’t explain why she had, either.

“Then why did you pretend that you didn’t?” Interpreting her silence as agreement, Rolf pulled at his hair in frustration.

“Rolf, please. I wasn’t making fun.” Taking his arm, she moved his hands clear of his hair and led him over to the chairs. Once they were seated, she firmly stated, “I’ve never heard the word pledge used that way before today.”

“Never?” That made him feel a little better. He thought.

“Not once.” She turned her hands palms up. “I’ve made academic pledges to my instructors.”

"Then..." He cleared his throat. "How do Water Fairies approach romance?" He *definitely* couldn't ask Jennings that!

"Most of us spend our first few hundred years at our studies. Romance, as such, comes later." She nodded very seriously in answer to his skeptical expression. "I could never have become a doctor this young if I hadn't worked very hard at it."

"I see."

"You do?" She took his hand and studied his eyes.

"'I'm beginning to, anyway." Sadly, he raised her hand to his lips. "I shouldn't have spoken about my feelings just now."

"I didn't mind." Especially not when he'd said something so nice. With a few days to ponder, and some more information about what exactly pledges were, she might get used to hearing things like that from him.

"Thank you." He released her hand and reached for his cane instead. "I do, in a way. I was prepared to suggest that we continue seeking out each other's company. That in time, we might both want more than friendship." Not that it mattered, since she wasn't interested. And wouldn't be, for approximately two hundred years.

Stunned, she stayed where she was as he rose.

"It's my own fault, of course." He tried to laugh, but it didn't come out right. It sounded more sad than anything. "All these weeks of living in your cities, eating your food, abiding by your customs—and it never occurred to me that this would be handled differently, too."

Every time he used the word 'your' it hit her heart like a hammer, breaking it into smaller and smaller pieces. They really were worlds apart, weren't they?

As her eyes filled with unshed tears, she offered quietly, "A most unfortunate misunderstanding."

"Unfortunate." He gripped the cane so tightly that the carving on the handle bit into his palm. "Yes. Quite so." She didn't even look at him. "At least we're still friends."

Her usually agile brain wobbled dizzily from thought to thought.

More than friendship.

Your customs.

Still friends.

"If you'll excuse me, I should go find Jennings." Bowing stiffly, he let himself out.

Imber let the tears come then, but they weren't the relief she'd expected. Her heart shuddered like a volcano nearing a devastating eruption.

Chapter 18

"Princess Constance?" The messenger lad knocked politely on the open door to further announce himself.

She held up a finger as she finished making a note. Smiled at him.

I'm never going to get this report finished with all of these interruptions. None of which are this lad's fault.

"I'm sorry to disturb you, Princess, but there's a Doctor Botere to see you."

"Doctor Botere?" She wrinkled her forehead, trying to place the name. She'd met with so many Water Fairy dignitaries since the announcement about the portals that it was impossible to keep track of them all. Had it really only been two weeks? It felt like two months, at least.

"Show the doctor in, please." Setting her quill aside, she smoothed her blue hair self-consciously. Every errand lately was 'of the utmost importance.'

Much to her surprise, a young Water Fairy entered the room and curtsied. The girl looked familiar, but was rather *too* young to have been part of the recent chaos. Appearances were deceptive after sixty, though.

"Thank you for seeing me, Your Highness."

Constance inclined her head, then motioned toward the other chair at the table.

"Won't you sit down, Doctor?"

"Thank you." Imber seated herself and folded her hands in her lap. "Lady Damaris sends her greetings and bids me ask if the Sky Fairy Tribe will accept an additional four hundred galdu folk."

Constance had to stop herself from frowning. This sort of request most often came via common messenger. Besides which, she had a funny feeling that the girl was connected with Mari somehow. *Lady Damaris*, she corrected herself. Her duties had her spending too much time with David, her former first officer, and she'd picked up his habit of using the familiar diminutive.

"Four hundred?" Constance toyed with a fresh quill. "We've already agreed to allot lands for ten thousand." She left the thought there, curious to see how the girl would answer.

"King Jasper is most gracious." Imber bowed slightly in her chair, causing Katilla's signal slip to crinkle in her pocket. The galdu had limited access to the signal stations now, a significant step forward.

She'd seized the signal as an opportunity to talk with a woman from the surface and now that she was here, she could feel her courage slipping away. But even the heartbeat of silence was too long for the perceptive Sky Fairy opposite her.

"Allow me to assure you that these families

boast some of the finest craftsfairies in the seven regions. In fact, we were hoping to persuade them to remain with us."

"Oh?" Intrigued, Constance did the opposite of what she wanted to. She leaned back. "I am curious, Doctor, that they didn't send a galdu representative to make this request."

Imber smiled. "Is not one fairy as good as another?" She and several other Water Fairies of prominent families were publically taking this stance to refute the notion that Water Fairies in general held themselves as superior.

Amused, Constance smiled as well. "I've always believed so."

"Would I be correct in reporting to Lady Damaris that you will consider the request?" Imber couldn't do it. Couldn't find a way to casually introduce the subject of surface romantic customs. What would she ask, anyway? And why? Rolf hadn't been near her since their falling out two weeks ago.

At least we're still friends. That's what he'd said, but clearly…

"Doctor?" Constance leaned forward this time. The girl hadn't heard a word she'd said. Something else was definitely afoot here.

"Yes?"

"Why are you really here?" Constance's curiosity went up several notches at the blush that rushed from the girl's modest collar to the roots of her severely pinned hair.

"I… What do you mean?" Imber affected ignorance in an attempt to deflect the scrutiny.

"I mean that I remember you from that night in Cundi." Constance tossed the quill she'd been playing with aside and made a mental leap aloud. "You're Rolf's friend." *Direct hit,* she congratulated herself as the girl's blush intensified.

Imber willed her cheeks to cool, but without success. "Yes, I am." What else could she possibly say?

A great feeling of sisterly concern welled up in Constance and she asked gently, "Is something troubling you, Imber?"

"Troubling me?" Imber started to brush the question aside. "Whatever do you mean?"

Constance arched an eyebrow. "You should never use the same feint twice, Doctor."

The frankness of the statement made Imber relax fractionally. "Am I so transparent?"

"It's easier to recognize the symptoms once you've had the disease," Constance teased lightly. "Does he know you care for him?"

Imber felt her cheeks drain of heat. "That's exactly the phrase he used," she murmured without thinking.

"The phrase *he* used?" Constance repeated for clarification. "Imber." She waited for the girl to look her in the eye. "What happened?"

"I'm not quite sure." Haltingly, Imber related the awkward experience in her carriage, finishing with, "So while I can't deny having feelings for him, is it any wonder that I am afraid to explore them?"

The door swung open before Constance could respond and Cambrian sauntered in.

"Hello." He smiled at them both as if he wasn't surprised to find someone with Constance.

The girl sitting across from Constance stared back at him, wide-eyed and pale. Paler than he'd ever seen a Water Fairy, which was saying a lot given that most of them had never felt the sun's touch.

"Cambrian." Constance stopped her husband in his tracks with a slight shake of her head. Her conversation with Imber was more important than any ten of the meetings she'd been in lately and she needed to finish it. "I'm sorry, darling, but this is a highly confidential conference. I'll have to ask you to wait outside."

"Of course. Forgive my intrusion." Bowing, he retreated, closing the doors behind him. Took his chin in his hand and tried to recall where he'd seen that girl before.

"You didn't have to do that." Imber appreciated it, though.

"He was just going to ask me to join him for lunch." Constance got up and walked around to Imber's side of the table. "Come here, Imber." She wrapped the hurting girl in a hug. "The world is full of misunderstandings. Small ones. Medium. Huge." Her hug must've squeezed a tear out, because one started trickling down Imber's cheek.

"We all have to learn to get along and it's a bumpy ride sometimes." Brushing the tear away, Constance smiled. "You should see me with Cambrian's mother, Queen Marta."

"But you…" Imber began to protest.

"We're both Sky Fairies?" Constance chuckled. "There are cultures and then there are subcultures, side-cultures, and," she waved a hand, "personalities and everything else. No matter who you are or how you were raised, there's always some subtlety you've overlooked or some nuance that escapes you."

"I suppose we've gotten very set in our ways after all this time." Imber sighed ruefully.

"Naturally." Constance shrugged. "Now, you have to decide if you want to be friends, or more, with Rolf going forward. And, you have to allow him to make the same decision."

"I think he already has." If he still wanted to be friends, he had a strange way of showing it.

"Ah, but we've learned that there are different ways of thinking, haven't we?" Constance patted her young friend lightly on the shoulder. "Rolf is not only a Silver Fairy, he's an historian. I can't speak for him and yet I wouldn't be at all surprised to find that he's locked in a state of indecision." She shook her head. "Sometimes I think he knows too much for his own good."

"Is that possible?" To Imber's Water Fairy sensibilities, that seemed a most peculiar idea.

"Why don't you go find out?" Cassidy gently pushed her toward the door.

Constance's words lingered with Imber as she meandered through Cachora after their meeting. She looked in shop windows without seeing the wares. Passed bakeries and eateries without smelling the food.

What did she want?

Abruptly, something struck her from the side, almost knocking her off her feet.

"Oh, I'm so sorry!" Strong hands steadied her. "Imber? Is that you?"

She looked up into an unfamiliar face under rowdy pink hair. The face was strangely weathered, as though it had seen hours and hours of sunshine and wind.

"Well of all the fairies to bump into after all this time." The man grinned down at her. "I understand congratulations are in order, too. You recently received your first title, if I've heard correctly?"

"Yes, I…" She still had no idea who he was.

"Now don't tell me. Let me think." He tapped a finger against his chin. "When you were little you wanted to be either a doctor of medicine or an aquatic botanist. I'd say you became a…"

She felt a mild irritation begin to grow within her as he studied her closely. Who was this man? Some long-lost relative?

"Doctor of medicine," she supplied just to have done with it. "Good day."

"Wait, wait." He caught her arm, then laughed as she stiffened. "You don't remember me, do you?" Releasing her, he produced a thin, flat pouch and flipped it open, revealing his identity papers. "Here, this should help."

She looked despite herself. "Inri Beech," she read aloud. That sounded so familiar. No, it *felt* familiar, like when she heard the name of one of her childhood friends. Her childhood? "Inri Beech?!" The name clicked in her memory at last. Their parents were good friends and Inri had often played with her or read to her when she was a child.

"Imber Botere." He opened his arms and she walked into them. "You have gotten so tall!"

She laughed. "That's what happens when you go away for fifty years!"

"Fifty… Has it been that long?" Inri whistled. "Hard to believe. Hey. Is there somewhere we can sit a while, talk and catch up?"

"Well." She was considering offering her carriage when he pointed to the restaurant behind her.

"I just got off a train and I am starving. How about it?"

"Alright." Why not? It would give her an excuse to put off her decision a while longer. It might even take her mind off of it altogether.

Inri was an animated conversationalist, often resorting to using his hands to demonstrate his adventures as a portal guard.

"I'd never seen one up close before," he tried to excuse the curiosity that nearly cost him his life, "so I just had to try sketching it."

"A mosquito. Really?" Imber shook her head in disbelief. "Even I know they're fearsome predators."

"It's a mistake I'll never make again." He grinned and rested his forearms on the table near the bowl he'd emptied of stew. Three times. "So. You're all grown up and a doctor already."

Something about the way he was watching her made her look down at her hands.

"What brings you to Cachora?" She glanced sideways at him. He obviously adored his position as a portal guard.

"My parents." He drew a figure-eight on the tabletop with one finger. "They think it's time for me to find a match."

"A m-match?" she stuttered. If she was too young for a pledge—which she now understood after talking with Constance—she was much, *much* too young for a match. That was the last step before marriage!

"That's what comes of hitting five hundred without so much as an attachment." Sighing, he waved to the waiter for their bill. "You're sure you don't want anything else?" He eyed her salad plate.

"No, thank you." She'd only ordered the salad so he wouldn't have to eat alone.

Inri paid the waiter and picked up his bag. "I don't think they expect me to marry right away." He returned to the previous subject. "Which is a good thing."

"Oh?" As they walked out of the restaurant, she had the terrible premonition that he was going to ask her if she was available.

"Yeah, because I'm not ready for marriage." He stuffed his free hand in the pocket of his jacket. "For one thing, I'm excited to visit the surface."

"You just finished fifty years as a portal guard. Isn't that enough for a while?" She could tell that the stories he'd shared were barely a peek into what he'd seen and done.

"That was nothing like this is going to be." He shook his head quickly. "All of Fairydom is opening up, Imber. I want to be there! I want to visit the cities. Talk to every fairy. Taste every kind of food."

"But what if you don't like it?" Frankly, she was both thrilled and terrified by his talk. She'd travelled the seven regions since childhood and felt very safe there. Why shouldn't she? The tunnels had no predators, the sea never ran out of food, and the only lightning was strictly controlled.

"Then I'll try a new city." He ran his fingers through his hair. "See? This is exactly what I expected. I'm never going to find a woman who wants to travel as much as I do."

She walked along in silence, thinking that over. It seemed ridiculously short-sighted for him to assume that all the available women in the seven regions would think precisely as she did.

"Here we are." Inri stared up at the luxurious, multi-colored calcite pillar where his parents lived.

"Indeed." Not liking the hopeful way he said 'we,' she started turning away even as she said, "It was good to see you. Thank you for…"

"Imber, couldn't you come up with me?" he pleaded. "At least let me introduce you to my parents as my attachment?"

"Your attachment?" Upset, she put a fist on her hip. "Inri Beech, if you think that's funny—"

"I'm completely serious." Dropping his bag on the steps, he held out both hands in an attempt to soothe her. "Hear me out. If they insist on my making a match, I'll never get to travel. But, if I've got an attachment who's too young for a match, they'll give me more time." He squinted at her. "You're what, seventy?"

"Seventy-seven," she corrected frostily.

"Perfect! Nobody would expect us to get married for a hundred years. Or even two." He grinned. "Meanwhile, you're free, too. You can pursue your education."

She cut him off. "I'm free right now, Inri. Don't try to make it sound like you'd be doing *me* a favor."

"Right." He sidled toward her. Time for a different tactic. "On the other hand, I used to think you liked me."

"So did I—fifty years ago, when I based my character assessments on how many books someone would read to me in one sitting." Of all the nerve!

His lips twitched. "You always were a cute little thing. Never knew you had such a temper, though." He reached for her and she sidestepped. "You'd love the surface." He tried getting closer and she moved away. "Ah, have a heart. One little kiss to see how you really feel about me."

"I'd rather kiss a hagfish," she hissed. With that, she spread her wings and flew off.

Hearing a rustle of wings behind her, she banked to her right and aimed for the nearest tunnel. She'd had a lot of practice at stopping short for a landing and even more with blending into a crowd from when she'd been helping to investigate the galdu councils.

Someone landed with her and a hand slipped into hers. *Not* Inri's rough, broad hand.

"Hi." Rolf kept his tone as nonchalant as he could.

"Rolf!" She lowered her voice when she saw how much attention her decision to fly had garnered. "What are you doing here?"

"Arranging with the Beeches to have a diplomatic party from the Plant Fairies stay with them."

"And they agreed?" The longer she'd stayed in Inri's company, the more she remembered about why her parents hadn't invited his parents over for the last few decades. With the passing years, they'd become unbearably haughty.

He slowed and stepped halfway behind her to make room for a passing delivery cart, his hand resting lightly on her waist for balance. Ignored his leaping pulse and resumed his position beside her. He also resumed holding her hand.

"Tentatively. I do think they were flattered by the invitation." He doubted they had the temperament for the job, but they did have plenty of spare rooms.

"They would be." She grimaced, not liking the spiteful sound to her words. "And you just decided to fly down instead of riding the hoist?" She suddenly noticed he wasn't carrying his cane. His leg didn't seem to be bothering him, either.

"Their primary concern was regarding the privacy of both groups." He tugged at his earlobe. "Ideally, my leaving via their window will convince them that surface fairies rarely have a use for hoists." Most of the time, in fact, a horsefly cart or even a small group of friends combined to aid those who couldn't fly on their own.

Anyway, the second he'd seen Imber with that stranger, he'd started trying to excuse himself. Taking the window was the fastest way to get to her. She'd seemed irritated at the end of her conversation, which made him feel a little better about seeing her with the handsome Water Fairy.

"Who was that you were talking with just now?"

"Someone I used to know." She didn't have to ask who he was referring to. Her question was how much Rolf had seen. Granted, Inri never even got close to his stated goal of a kiss, but from above their step-and-counter-step had to have looked peculiar.

"Oh." That didn't sound as if she was planning to see him again, which lifted Rolf's spirits. Despite what happened—or didn't happen—in her carriage, he couldn't seem to help his feelings for her. "I hope you don't mind."

"No, but the city guards might. Technically, flying is restricted to certain parts of the city at very definite times and…" Her words trailed off as he silently raised their joined hands. It felt so natural to be holding his hand that she hadn't thought twice about it.

"Come with me." She pulled on his hand, guiding him into one tunnel after another. Stopped at the entrance to a smallish chamber.

"Wow." Rolf walked further inside. It wasn't a large chamber as they went, but he liked that it was open, with no buildings to block his view. "This is amazing."

"I used to play here when I was younger." She hopped onto one of the balance beams and walked across it, arms folded across her chest. The seashell slides, the swings, even the driftwood 'tree' she used to climb. It all looked exactly as she remembered it. Only much shorter.

"And you brought me here today because?" It would make a good place to talk, he'd give her that. They were the only fairies in the whole chamber.

"Because the last time we talked, you didn't let me finish."

His eyebrows shot up to his hairline. "I didn't let you finish?"

"That's right." Her pulse spiked when he came toward her. "I was in the middle of a thought and you interrupted." Her heart sank when he stopped a few twigs away and put his hands in his pockets.

"I must be terribly boorish." He couldn't guess where she was going with this, but he hoped they got there soon. He hadn't enjoyed this conversation the first time, either.

Chapter 19

"Have you been thinking about it?" She needed him to come closer. Her own legs were trembling traitorously and she'd never make it over to him.

"Of course I've thought about it." He shifted a quarter turn away from her. "What kind of a question is that?"

"A direct one." He still didn't look at her. Desperate, she began pulling the pins out of her hair.

"Imber?" Concerned, he closed the distance between them in two long strides, then captured her hands and held them fast. Since she was still standing on the plank or whatever it was, she was almost as tall as he was. "What are you doing?"

"This." She kissed him. And—it was like the time her teacher brought a sample of weak lightning into the class for them to experiment with. Only more so.

"Imber." He cupped her face in his hands, amazed at how steady they were when his insides were jumping like tadpoles on a warm summer night. She'd spoiled her hairdo just to get his attention and he thought she'd never looked lovelier. "You didn't have to do that."

"I know." Slipping her arms around his

waist, she rested her head on his shoulder. A few displaced pins poked awkwardly and she shifted to a more comfortable position. "Rolf, I didn't know that a pledge was sort of like an attachment."

"A what?" He drew back to look down at her.

"And you don't know what an attachment is." She wrinkled her nose playfully at him. "See? We weren't disagreeing, we just weren't communicating."

"I'm willing to try again if you are." He brushed his lips across hers. Tightened his hold when she began to pull away.

"I can't talk like this," she whispered, keenly aware of how easy it would be to kiss him again.

Conceding the point, he put a little distance between them and allowed her to lead him to a semi-soft spot on the sand beneath the driftwood 'tree.' It was a delightfully informal place for them to discuss specific points of their cultures in peace and quiet, something he'd had too little of lately.

"An attachment is when two Water Fairies decide they would rather be in each other's company than in anybody else's." She drew a 'one plus one equals two' in the sand. "Though they may change their minds, it is considered the first official phase of a relationship."

"An official phase, hmm?" Rolf cleared his throat to keep himself from laughing. When was he going to learn how little he knew about Water Fairies? "That is something like a pledge," he admitted. "But if you didn't know what they were, how is that you know now?"

Amused, she admitted, "Constance was kind enough to explain them to me."

"Ah." He made a mental note to thank Constance for explaining pledges to Imber. They weren't overly complicated, he just got a little tongue-tied whenever he thought about putting them and Imber in the same sentence.

"I think your tradition of pledge gifts is very romantic."

"Sometimes." He chuckled. "I know of one poor fellow, an apprentice blacksmith, who made a complete set of sewing tools for the woman he was interested in."

"Sewing tools? But why?" That didn't sound the least bit romantic.

"Because she was a marvelous seamstress and he wanted her to have the best tools for her work." Rolf still felt sorry for him.

"I…see." Imber dredged up the courage to ask, "What happened?"

"She politely refused the gift," Rolf smiled, "then told him she would still consider the pledge if he wished to try again."

"That was quite generous of her," Imber decided aloud.

"Well, it helped that they loved each other dearly." He stroked her loose hair softly so as not to disturb the remaining hair pins.

"Then how…?" She bit her lip. Was that an impolite question?

"How could he make such an unromantic gift?" Rolf shrugged. "Neither of them were perfect. I've often thought that their relationship is the stronger for his mistake. He knows she'll be honest with him and she knows he'll listen to her."

"I never would've thought of it that way," Imber admitted.

"Truthfully, I didn't think of it on my own, either." He lowered his voice to a whisper and confided, "That's the story of my mother's cousin's son."

She laughed and snuggled a little closer. "The main thing then is that they communicated."

"True." He quirked an eyebrow at her. "Don't you want to know what he got her for his second attempt?"

"Yes, very much."

"He asked his master to make a silver bracelet for her. Then, he carved their names together on one side and promised to inscribe the other side with the names of each of their children."

"I'm starting to see why she said yes." Imber's heart melted at the sweetly sentimental—and incredibly brave—gift.

What would Rolf give for a gift? The question

was in her mind before she knew it was coming.

She coughed to clear the emotions from her throat and casually remarked, "They must have been older to be so advanced in their crafts."

"Actually, most surface fairies have settled on a trade or occupation of one sort or another by the time they're approaching their first century."

"So early?" She was genuinely surprised. She intended to study two more subjects and achieve the title of scholar before settling on an occupation, as did most of her peers.

"Many will change occupations during their life," he explained. "Take Jennings, for example. He was a windfairy in the Sky Fairy Royal Fleet for…I don't know how long. Now he's Prince Cambrian's valet."

"That has to be an interesting story." She laughed and laced her fingers through his. "He seems like a good friend, too."

"Yes, he is." Rolf rested his cheek against her hair. "He's told me every day since our, um, miscommunication that I should go talk to you again."

She waited a moment before asking, "Why didn't you?"

"Oh, I had a dozen excuses. I was leaving. You were staying. You didn't want to talk about it." He sighed and squeezed her hand gently. "And when I couldn't think of an excuse, there was always something to be done.

A flying lesson to help teach, a meeting to attend, or, of course, my history book to update."

"I missed you." She held her breath while she waited for his response.

His eyes closed and he pressed a kiss to her forehead. "I missed you, too."

A feeling of supreme contentment washed over her as she listened to his heart beating in his chest.

"I wish I'd known about this chamber sooner."

"Why is that?" His chuckle rumbled through him, making her smile.

"It's a great place to hide from the messengers and councilors and," he sighed, "everyone else that expects me to help them rearrange the face of Fairydom."

"At least you're not a prince." She patted his chest. "I don't know when Cambrian finds time to sleep."

"No, that's true." He cleared his throat. "However, as an historian, I can legally mediate between two tribes. As the only historian in the seven regions who hasn't been erroneously recorded as deceased," he grimaced to himself, "I can scarcely sit down to update my book before someone else calls for me."

She straightened away and looked at him, eyes wide. "You can mediate between tribes but you can't offer a pledge gift?"

"Mediating sounds more important than it is." He rubbed the back of his neck, seeing her point. "The two scenarios are governed by very different laws. Surprisingly, there's less responsibility in conveying messages or sitting in council than there is in making an eight- or ten-thousand year commitment." Getting to his feet, he slapped the sand off his trousers, careful not to send any her direction.

"Yes, I hadn't thought of it that way." She cocked her head to one side. "You speak of being an historian as if it were not a lifelong commitment."

"It can be." He offered her his hands and pulled her to her feet. "Truthfully, though, many historians are retired, oh," he verbally plucked occupations from the air, "farmers or craftsfairies or even Wranglers. In a thousand years or so, I may do the reverse."

"Hmm." She stayed close to him a moment longer than necessary, then withdrew to dust herself off. "What would you do?"

"I guess I'd like to try building windships. Or flying them."

"Flying them where?" She brushed her hands together to remove the last of the sand.

"Where?" He grinned despite the seriousness of the question. "All over Fairydom. Who knows what that will look like in a thousand years? The kings have already removed restrictions on colonizing near the

West Sea and up near your mountain portals. We may even expand beyond the known surface borders."

"That sounds amazing." Loving the excitement in his voice, she wished she had some excuse for hugging him.

"There's no telling which way the future will jump, as my great-great grandfather says." He held out his arm and was glad when she came to stand beside him. "So." He kissed her forehead and the tip of her nose. "Friends?"

The husky note in his voice sent shivers down her spine. "Friends." She sealed the promise with a soft kiss.

Reluctantly, they left the little haven, hand in hand. Their aimless wandering may have contributed to how long it took for them to be found and they enjoyed every moment.

"Historian!" A messenger lass nearly ran into them when they stopped at her hail. "Councilor Naydie requests your presence."

"Where is she?" Rolf accepted a slip of paper from the messenger lass as the answer to his question and pressed a llow into her hand. "Here. Don't be late, but find something to eat or drink to refresh yourself, alright?"

"Thank you!" The lass was off in a flash.

"You didn't have to do that." Imber was impressed at the gesture, though. "She receives food and drink as part of her job."

"The poor girl probably ran her short legs

off trying to find me." Rolf shrugged boyishly. "Anyway, it was worth it to see her smile."

"Doctor Botere?" A deep, booming voice turned heads toward them—or at least, toward the middle-aged Water Fairy man beaming at Imber. "Is that really you?"

"Yes, it's me." Imber hugged him happily. "How are you doing, Grandfather?"

The messenger lass forgotten, Rolf suddenly couldn't seem to stand up straight enough.

"I'm well, my dear." Her grandfather patted her shoulder. "How are you? And who is your friend?"

Imber colored beautifully but obediently introduced, "Grandfather, this is Historian Rolf Warner."

"Ah, the fellow who stirred up such a ruckus in Lauga."

"I had some help with that, sir." Rolf's own cheeks flushed as he lifted his palms in Water Fairy fashion, showing that they were empty.

"Yes, the ex-baron. It's a dark day in the seven regions when a title is stripped from a fairy." Grandfather shook his head sorrowfully. "I have to take partial responsibility for what happened, I'm afraid."

"Grandfather?" Imber couldn't believe her ears. "You? Why?"

"Hmm? Why? Well, because it was I who recommended him for his first doctorate."

Now he clucked his tongue, presumably at himself. "I thought I saw greatness in that young man. A gift for leadership."

"You shouldn't blame yourself, sir." Rolf didn't. "He *did* have a gift for leadership. He simply chose to squander it on a malicious cause."

"You're too kind." Grandfather eyed Rolf with a new interest. "I say, I'd very much like to sup with you, Historian. Hear your tales and find out how it is that one so young is also so wise."

"Duty calls at the moment, sir." Rolf smiled. "But if that's an open invitation, I'd be pleased to join you when I can."

"Excellent." Grandfather pounded the tunnel floor once with his cane for emphasis. "I'll send word to, um…"

"The Parota," Imber supplied, remembering the meal she'd declined to attend with Katilla and the others.

"I look forward to it, sir." With a final, carefully guarded look at Imber, Rolf bowed slightly and… Wait, he didn't know where he was going.

Opening the paper he was thankfully still holding onto, he silently read, "Come to the quium."

"Rolf?" Imber touched his arm. "What is it?"

"This summons." He showed her the paper.

"I don't know where the quium is."

"You better go along, my dear." Grandfather smiled and dropped a sly wink at them both. "Make sure he doesn't get lost." The older man did an about-face and meandered away, whistling softly.

"Don't mind him." Imber sighed rather than blush. "He fancies himself a matchmaker."

"I don't mind at all." Rolf offered his elbow, which she took.

Despite the very real temptation to take the long way, Imber very properly showed him the shortest path—only to find that she was needed as well!

"We've had messengers out looking for you two for over an hour," remarked a disgruntled councilor.

"My apologies." Rolf seated Imber, then himself, at the large, round table. "We came as soon as we heard."

Constance and Cambrian exchanged apparently innocent looks, then he cleared his throat.

"Rolf, we've just had an update from my father." Cambrian couldn't explain how the message came, only that he had it. "The shrub roots are flexing."

Rolf gaped at him. "This early?"

Cambrian nodded and rose, prompting Rolf to do the same. He hadn't said a word about what the news might mean. He wanted an unbiased second opinion and, as the resident historian, Rolf was the best fairy to get it from.

"He's had the same reports from five different locations." Cambrian used a long pointer to indicate the spots on the map of the surface that Dixon, the Sky Fairy navigator from Captain Watts' crew, had enlarged for them. "We're anticipating an early spring."

"Have we established direct contact with the Silver Fairy Tribe yet?" Rolf fumbled for the pointer on his side of the table. He hoped he was wrong.

"We have." Councilor Naydie watched with considerable interest as Rolf drew an imaginary set of lines between the five points with the tip of his pointer.

He stopped and looked at Cambrian. "Could this be a repeat of the Failed Spring?" he asked grimly.

"I'd like to say no." Cambrian leaned both fists on the table.

"What is this you speak of?" Naydie's eyebrows drew in and she looked sharply between the two men.

"Spring once came so early in the mountains that the lands below were still frozen. The melting snow rushed upon the lowlands, where it froze on top and dripped into tunnels below. Some ran off into the sea, but not enough." Rolf slowly set the pointer down. "Eventually, tunnels flooded, lives were lost, and resources spoiled."

"Many Sky Fairies died trying to clear the skies of clouds so the sun could dry the lowlands." Constance's voice, usually cheery or at least crisp, came out as grave as a funeral march.

"When was this tragedy?" Naydie didn't sound like herself, either.

"The new generation that survived the Failed Spring has since passed." Cambrian resumed his seat. "And not for another half a generation have we seen spring arrive so early."

Naydie shook her head, not familiar with his terms.

"Fifteen thousand years, Councilor." Rolf took his chair again, also. "It happened fifteen thousand years ago."

A low murmur ran around the room, causing Rolf to prick his ears. But he didn't understand enough of Margua, the Water Fairy language, to know what was being said. There was a flurry of motion, including four messengers racing out of the room, then silence.

Imber's hand stole into his and squeezed it reassuringly.

"It's possible that this won't be as bad." Cambrian hand-shrugged. "Winter was late this year. Perhaps the snow is not so deep as then."

"It was late because the pirates were stormpiling the clouds," Constance reminded him flatly. "Captain Watts and his crew barely survived the storm they helped unleash."

"In short, we cannot be certain what is coming. A boon of early warmth, a longer growing season—or catastrophe," Cambrian concluded grimly.

"I strongly recommend reaching out to each tribe." Rolf's troubled eyes roved the map. He didn't even know where his grandparents were. They'd laughed about touring Fairydom, something they'd never had time to enjoy doing as the former king and queen of their tribe. "Ask them to evaluate the signs. Warn them about what may be coming."

"A year ago, that wouldn't have been possible." Cambrian's face twisted in a wry smile. "We, too, ask that you take these steps."

A frail, white-haired man rested his forearms on the table. "Young men," amusement twinkled in his eyes, "we have already begun doing so. For too long we have failed to fill the full measure of our tribal responsibilities. In the case of this past catastrophe you spoke of, we failed you because of our ignorance. Going forward, we will have no such excuse. Nor shall we want it."

Coming to himself, Rolf grabbed quill and ink. Accepted a blank page from the alert Imber and began scribbling the historic words for all he was worth.

"We will not wait to be reunited to do our part." Sighing as if in weariness, the elderly man motioned to another councilor.

"We have also sent word to our outposts." A much younger woman came forward to stand by his chair. "In a matter of hours, the liquid water on the surface will fall to half that of its present level. Should the warming weather prove to be a disaster, we are prepared to reduce the surface water by half again."

The eldest galdu in the room came slowly to his feet. "And we will see to it that word of your prompt action is carried beyond this room to the ears of every galdu in the seven regions. This will heal many hearts." He bowed deeply to the Water Fairy speakers.

Rolf noted the names that he knew and jotted down a short description of the galdu speaker so he could ask Katilla about him later. Sketched the room and its occupants in brief detail. Pictures weren't often included in histories, but he felt the occasion warranted it.

After a long night of writing and sketching, he blinked in confusion at an empty plate on the table beside a stack of his papers. Well. It wasn't exactly empty. There were plenty of crumbs and a crumpled napkin on it.

"Where did that come from?" he wondered aloud.

"The kitchen." Imber chuckled and added it to a stack of identical plates. "You certainly were hungry."

A quick glance around the table showed a

few others performing the same service and Rolf felt all the more ridiculous for not having noticed a thing going on around him that wasn't related to history.

"I, um, get this way sometimes. When I'm working."

"I noticed." Imber handed the plates and things off to a waiter. Leaned against the edge of the table.

"That's the first time I've eaten a sandwich in the middle of it, though." He hesitated. "If that's what it was."

"You must be improving." She tapped the tip of his nose lightly. "You don't have to apologize, Rolf."

"I don't? I mean," he rubbed ink-stained fingers together, "I forgot about everything except what I was doing."

"You don't. I promise." She smiled warmly. "I admire your dedication."

"My dedication?" Laughing, he rose to stretch. Caught hold of the table. "My leg's asleep." He shook it vigorously, gritting his teeth against the prickles of pain shooting through it.

"I'm not surprised." Looping her arm through his, she aimed them at the door. "Let's walk awhile. They've adjourned for now."

"Right." He blew out a breath and shook his head. "They deserve a break."

"They do? What about you?"

"Me?" Rolf reached up to run his fingers through his hair. "I'm just an historian. In a couple of generations, nobody will even remember I was here."

"Your descendants will." She smiled and tried hard not to blush.

"I like the sound of that." He pressed a kiss to her cheek.

Hand in hand, they walked away from the chaos, happy just to be together.

Author's Notes

Advena: Fairies and their descendants from the surface detained by the Water Fairy Tribe
Origin: Advenæ: Latin: foreigners
Bilera: Water Fairy place of meeting
Origin: Basque: meeting
Botere clan: Oldest and most powerful Water Fairy clan
Origin: Basque: one definition is "potential"
Cachora: the capitol city of the Water Fairy Tribe. (*Pronounced Cash-ora*)
Origin: Cachoeira, Portuguese for *waterfall*
Cocheta: Stranger
Origin: www.warpaths2peacepipes.com/native-american-indian-names/native-american-names-c.htm
Domesticated animals: I have imagined a world where there are cows, goats, etc., that are small enough for farmers roughly one-quarter inch tall to raise and tend.
Mugan region: The seventh Water Fairy region, nearest the exits to the surface; settled anciently by the wealthiest and most powerful clans. Water Fairy territory is arranged in circles, going out like ripples from Muina, the central region.
Origin: Basque: Border.
Zaldun: Water Fairy for guardian and protector
Origin: Basque: Knight

www.ingramcontent.com/pod-product-compliance
Lightning Source LLC
Chambersburg PA
CBHW071233190726
48292CB00007B/2261